EYEBEAM: RENDER UNTO PEACHES

by Sam Hurt

Other books by Sam Hurt:
I'm Pretty Sure I've Got My Death-Ray in Here Somewhere!
Eyebeam, Therefore I Am
Eenie Meenie Minie Tweed
Our Eyebeams Twisted
The Mind's Eyebeam
Eyebeam: Teetering on the Blink

Texas Monthly Press
P.O. Box 1569
Austin, Texas 78767

A B C D E F G H

Printed in the U.S.of A.

Attention Seekers of the Beam and individual Beamofanatics: Keep up with *Eyebeam* through New Stream Comics, P.O. Box 893, Austin, Texas 78767. Contact Chuck Higdon (512) 343-0418.

Library of Congress Cataloging-in-Publication Data

Hurt, Sam
Eyebeam, render unto Peaches / by Sam Hurt.
p. cm.
ISBN 0-87719-115-8 (pbk.) : $6.95
I. Title
PM 6728.E94H85 1988 88-20052
741.5'973—dc19 CIP

Thanks to Tom Hurt for actually experiencing the middle of page 48. Thanks to John Hurt for pages 7, 14, 19, 36, 48, 61, 69, 83, 94, 107, 111, 114, and books 1 through 4. Just Kidding. Thanks to Chris Ware and J. Keen for technical assistance in coloring the back cover and for bringing beer. Thanks to Billy Mangham for the sleeping dog on page 87. This book is respectfully rendered unto Yasuko and the little Onigiri-chan.

Eyebeam: Render Unto Peaches

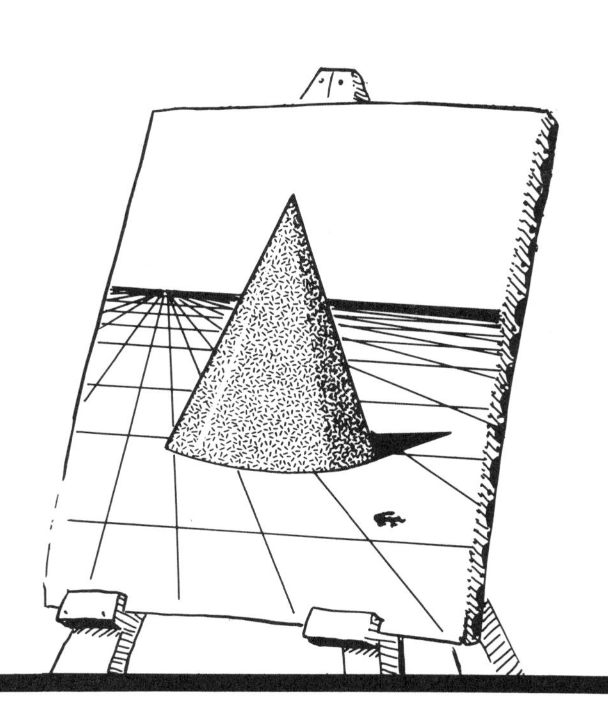

EYEBEAM
CAUTION: WET CEMENT
PEACE
LOVE

ACE
EQUIPMENT RENTAL

BUMP.
RUSTLE.
SLIDE

HEY, SALLY– DID YOU EAT ALL THE PEANUT BUTTER?
NO.

RUSTLE.
CLICK.
SLIDE.
OPEN.
CLOSE.

SLIDE
RUSTLE
OPEN
CLOSE
CLICK
UNCLICK
SLIDE
BUMP
MAYBE THEY **CAN** BE TRAINED...

THROUGHOUT HISTORY, THEY HAVE TRIED IN PRIMITIVE WAYS TO WORSHIP US.
WE BRING YOU GOLD AND RUBIES, O RAK.

EACH GENERATION CREATES MORE ELABORATE FORMS OF ADULATION, AND STILL THEY FAIL TO HONOR US PROPERLY.
THE CAT STUFF STORE
NO PETS

...BUT YOU HAVE TO ADMIT, THEY DID A PRETTY GOOD JOB WITH THESE NIGHT-PEDESTALS
THAT'S TRUE.

HAVE YOU NOTICED? YOU DON'T SEE RATLIFF AROUND MUCH LATELY.
YOU'RE RIGHT– ONCE YOU COULD ALMOST ALWAYS FIND HIM WHEREVER YOU SAW HIM LAST.

I GUESS THAT'S WHY HE ALWAYS REMINDED ME OF A BEAN-BAG CHAIR...
HE MUST'VE FOUND SOME NEW HOBBY THAT'S EATING UP ALL HIS TIME.

YOU KNOW WHAT I LIKE ABOUT BREAKFAST, BETH? BREAKFAST IS THE FIRST MEAL IN THE REST OF YOUR LIFE!
RATLIFF, YOU'RE ONE OF THE FEW MEN ON EARTH WHO CAN LOOK VIRILE IN A NIGHTSHIRT...
TOASTER YUMS!
EGG McTOASTER

EYEBEAM

TONIGHT ON "NIGHTLINE"- HAS THE GOVERNMENT BEEN CONDUCTING SECRET EXPERIMENTS ON THE MILITARY APPLICATIONS OF STEROIDS? OUR GUEST, DR. TADDUN LIKELY...
ABC NEWS
©87 Sam Hurt

NOW, DR. LIKELY, THESE ARE VERY SERIOUS CHARGES YOU'RE MAKING. WHAT KIND OF EVIDENCE DO YOU HAVE?
EVIDENCE? TED, JUST LOOK AT THE SIZE OF MY **HEAD**...

-Y!KES-
I THOUGHT IT WAS OUR DYNAMIC VISUAL FORMAT...
...AND **SPEAKING** OF BIG HEADS...

GOOD AFTERNOON, EYEBEAM...
RATLIFF! -WE HAVEN'T SEEN YOU AROUND FOR A WHILE...

REALLY? COME TO THINK OF IT, I GUESS I'VE BEEN SPENDING A LOT OF TIME WITH BETH LATELY.
OH, YEAH! -I FORGOT YOU TWO HAVE A THING GOING ON! TELL ME- HOW'S THAT BEEN GOING?

OH, NEVER MIND!

-SLIDE
-RUSTLE
-BUMP

WE DEFINITELY HAVE PEANUT BUTTER, RIGHT?
RIGHT.

-CLICK
-SLIDE
-SLIDE
-SLIDE
-SLAM
-SHUFFLE
-BUMP

EYEBEAM

?
Sam Hurt
©87

I'M GOING TO RETRACE MY STEPS UNTIL I FIND OUT WHERE I LEFT THOSE DARN KEYS...

!

AK!

MY LIFE SURE HAS CHANGED SINCE I'VE BEEN INVOLVED WITH BETH. I'M FINALLY GETTING USED TO IT THOUGH...

AT FIRST, IT WAS ALL SO NEW, SO INTENSE– I WAS BLINDED BY MY EMOTIONS...

THINGS ARE A LITTLE CLEARER NOW– I CAN ENJOY IT MORE...
RATLIFF, SOME FAMILY BUSINESS HAS COME UP... I HAVE TO LEAVE TOWN INDEFINITELY.
©87 Sam Hurt

WHAT HAPPENED? WHERE DID EVERYTHING GO?
WILL YOU MISS ME?

I'M SORRY YOU HAVE TO GO, BETH. HAVE A NICE TRIP...
WILL YOU MISS ME?

WILL I **MISS** YOU? EACH TICK OF THE CLOCK WILL POUND AT MY HEAD LIKE AN OBNOXIOUS ASPIRIN COMMERCIAL... EACH MINUTE WILL LURCH BY LIKE THE MOON DRAGGING THROUGH ITS PHASES. I'LL BE ALONE WITH THE TORMENTED RAVINGS OF THE DARKEST RECESSES OF MY OWN SOUL...
©87 Sam Hurt

YOU WILL BE CREATING ONE MAN'S PRIVATE LITTLE **HECK**...
OH, RATLIFF! YOU ALWAYS KNOW THE RIGHT THING TO SAY...

EYEBEAM
WHAT DO I DO? MY GIRLFRIEND JUST LEFT TOWN... HOW DO I DEAL WITH THIS ?

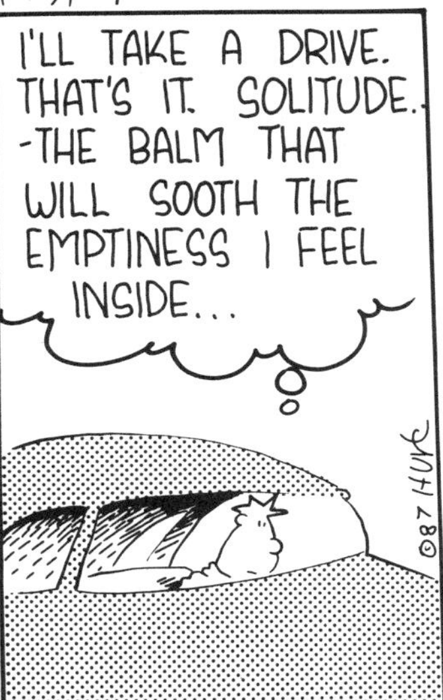
I'LL TAKE A DRIVE. THAT'S IT. SOLITUDE. -THE BALM THAT WILL SOOTH THE EMPTINESS I FEEL INSIDE...

YES! SOLITUDE. I'M ON THE ROAD TO INNER PEACE- THE ROAD TO SELF-RELIANCE.

I DON'T SUPPOSE IT WOULD HURT TO STOP-OFF ON THE WAY, THOUGH...
CLUB MEAT

EYEBEAM

FOR YEARS, I'VE BEEN COMING TO THESE PLACES, TRYING TO MEET GIRLS.
CLUB MEAT
©87 HUK

IT WAS ALWAYS A MISERABLE EXERCISE IN FAILURE. BUT NOW THAT I HAVE A GIRLFRIEND, I THOUGHT I MIGHT ENJOY BEING HERE WITHOUT TRYING TO MEET ANYBODY...

UH... HI. UH, WELL I'VE NEVER DONE THIS BEFORE, BUT YOU LOOK LIKE SOMEONE I'D REALLY LIKE TO KNOW...

WHERE WERE YOU DURING MY LONELY HOUR OF DESPAIR?
I DON'T KNOW, BUT THERE'S A GOOD CHANCE I WAS STUCK IN TRAFFIC SOMEWHERE...

WHAT'S THE MATTER, RATLIFF? YOU LOOK STEAMED...
I MET THIS GIRL. SHE'S BRIMMING OVER WITH CHUNKS OF LUSCIOUSNESS..!

BUT...? OH, I SEE- YOU CAN'T TAKE ADVANTAGE OF THE SITUATION BECAUSE OF BETH...
WHAT KIND OF SYSTEM IS THIS, ANYWAY?
©87 HUK

IT'S FEAST OR FAMINE AT THE TABLE OF LOVE. EITHER YOU DO WITHOUT, OR YOU'RE FORCED TO LET VAST QUANTITIES OF SURPLUS GO TO WASTE...
DARNIT, EYEBEAM, IT'S TIME FOR SOMEONE TO INVENT THE TUPPERWARE OF LOVE...

EYEBEAM
BOY! FATE SURE HAS A WEIRD SENSE OF TIMING...
...FOR THE FIRST TIME IN MY LIFE, I HAVE A GIRLFRIEND, AND THE MINUTE SHE LEAVES TOWN, BANG! -I MEET ANOTHER BEAUTIFUL WOMAN WHO WANTS TO GET TO KNOW ME...
©87 Sambo

THERE'S JUST ONE THING I'D LIKE TO KNOW...

...WHY DOES THIS KIND OF MANURE ALWAYS HAVE TO HAPPEN TO ME?
OH, IT'S YOU!

HI, RATLIFF. WHERE HAVE YOU BEEN?
I'D RATHER NOT TALK ABOUT IT.
©87 Sam Hurt

NO! YOU WENT OUT WITH THAT OTHER GIRL?! WHY, YOU SLY DOG, YOU!
WHY COULDN'T I HAVE LEFT WELL ENOUGH ALONE?

OH. SELF-REPROACHFUL, HUH? SO, I TAKE IT YOU...
YES. FOR OVER TWO HOURS...

WHY, YOU MARATHON SLED DOG YOU...
I COULDN'T HELP IT- WE HELD HANDS LIKE THERE WAS NO TOMORROW!

GREAT. AFTER A LIFETIME OF SEARCHING, I FINALLY FIND A GIRLFRIEND- THEN I RUN OFF AND HOLD HANDS WITH THE FIRST HOT CHICK WHO COMES ALONG
©87 Sam Hurt

FUNNY- I ALWAYS THOUGHT BEING A BUTT-KING WOULD MAKE ME FEEL LIKE A BIG SHOT. INSTEAD, I FEEL ALL ALONE... DISTANT FROM EVERYTHING ELSE. THE WHOLE WORLD IS JUST A SPECK ON THE HORIZON...

THAT'S FUNNY. I THOUGHT RATLIFF WAS IN HERE...
SIGH...

WHAT YOU HAVE TO DO, EYEBEAM, IS TO GET RID OF ANYTHING YOU HAVEN'T USED IN THE LAST YEAR...
AWWW...

...OTHERWISE, YOU WIND UP BURIED IN YOUR OWN STUFF, LIKE RATLIFF...
BUT I HAVE A LOT OF THINGS I DON'T USE, BUT I LIKE TO HAVE AROUND.
©87 Sam Hurt

YOU HAVE TO BE RUTHLESS, OR YOUR POSSESSIONS WIND UP RULING YOU...
...LIKE THIS, FOR EXAMPLE. IT'S NEAT, SALLY!

OK: DID YOU USE IT IN THE LAST YEAR?
WELL, NO, BUT-

RATLIFF... I'M BACK!
SHE'S BACK! THE MOMENT I'VE BEEN YEARNING FOR YET DREADING...
OH, BETH! I'VE BEEN SO BAD- SO UNWORTHY OF YOUR LOVE! I DON'T DESERVE YOU...
HERE. GET UP. IT CAN'T BE THAT BAD. WE'RE ALL HUMAN...
FORGIVENESS! A SWEET SYMPHONY TO MY SOUL! I AM MADE WHOLE AGAIN!
SO TELL ME WHAT DID YOU DO TO MAKE YOU FEEL SO GUILTY?
UH... LET'S SEE... DOUBLE PARKING... CHEATING ON CROSSWORDS.. STUFF LIKE THAT...
I NEED TO GET AWAY FOR A WHILE... I THINK I'LL FIRE UP THE OLD TIME MACHINE.
THE CAUSAL CHAIN OF HISTORY: YOU BREAK IT, YOU BUY IT.
TIME MACHINE
©87 Sam Hurt NEW STREAM COMICS
I'LL HEAD FOR A TIME WHEN LIFE WAS SIMPLER... BEFORE HOME COMPUTERS; BEFORE TELEVISION; EVEN BEFORE RADIO!
BEFORE CALIBRATED INSTRUMENTS. OOPS.
HEY, DUDE- LONG TIME, NO BRACHIATE!

HOWDY, STRANGER.
HI. YOU KNOW, I'M SURPRISED I CAN UNDERSTAND YOU.

WHAT'S TO UNDERSTAND? I CAME; I SAW; I ATE!
PERHAPS SPOKEN LANGUAGE IS MORE CONSTANT THAN WRITTEN. -THEN WRITTEN DOCUMENTS WOULDN'T SHOW HOW FAR BACK THE THREADS OF MODERN LANGUAGE ACTUALLY STRETCH...
©87 Sam Hurt

THREADS? CHECK THESE- LITERALLY THE CAT'S PAJAMAS!
AHA! SO YOU DO SPEAK AN ANCIENT TONGUE!

EYEBEAM

WHERE'S RATLIFF, EYEBEAM? I HAVEN'T SEEN HIM AROUND...
WELL, HE SAID HE NEEDED TO GET AWAY FOR A WHILE. MAYBE HE TOOK A LITTLE VACATION...
©87 Sam Hurt

HE PROBABLY HAS MORE STRESS THAN HE'S USED TO THESE DAYS...
WHEREVER HE IS, I HOPE HE'S GETTING A GOOD REST...

SO WHEN THE MASTADON COMES AROUND THE BEND, YOU SHOUT, "HEY"! AND HE FALLS OFF THE CLIFF...
YEAH... OR WE COULD DO A BIG SALAD INSTEAD...

AH-HA!
WHAT IS IT, EYEBEAM?
INSTRUMENTS
SCIENTIFIC EQUIPMENT

I FIGURED OUT WHERE RATLIFF WENT, SALLY. ACCORDING TO MY INSTRUMENTS, HE'S VISITING THE DISTANT PAST IN MY TIME MACHINE...
HMMM... SOUNDS LIKE A TRIP THAT COULD PROVE EDUCATIONAL...
©87 Sam Hurt

I KNOW IT SOUNDS CORNY, BUT I GUARANTEE IT'S A LINE THE BABES WILL GO FOR EVERY TIME!
"DARLING, YOU AND I ARE TWO STICKS, AND FATE IS RUBBING US TOGETHER"...?

YOU KNOW WHAT I COULD GO FOR?... A GOOD PIZZA!
NOW, WHO COULD THAT BE?
DING
DONG

DING-DONG
MAYBE IT'S THAT PIZZA I WAS WISHING FOR. UNLIKELY. A: THIS IS THE REAL WORLD. B: IT'S MONDAY. MORE LIKELY, IT'S THE OPPOSITE...
DING
DONG
NEW STREAM COMICS
©87 Sam Hurt

...DOOR TO DOOR SOLICITATION
I FEEL A NEED HERE, TIM.
THAT'S WHY WE WERE LED HERE, JAMMY...

EXEBEAM

I THINK WE CAN DO A LOT OF GOOD HERE, TIM...
WE WERE DRAWN HERE, JAMMY. I SENSE A DEEP NEED...

THE PEOPLE WHO LIVE HERE- THEY LOOK LOST... EMPTY. MY HEART JUST GOES OUT TO THEM...
THEIR EMPTINESS COMES FROM LEADING MEANINGLESS LIVES...

WITHOUT THE OPPORTUNITY TO GIVE, LIFE **HAS** NO MEANING!
WE'LL GIVE THEIR LIVES ALL THE MEANING THEY CAN AFFORD...

AND SO, I MUST BID YOU FAREWELL, MY SIMPLE AND PRIMITIVE FRIEND...
SAME TO YOU, DUDE.

I HAVE GAINED A SENSE OF THE "ONENESS" OF MANKIND... IT'S BEEN ONE OF THE MOST FASCINATING EPISODES OF MY ENTIRE LIFE...
IT'S BEEN... REAL.

CLASP
GRASP

I SHALL CARRY THESE MEMORIES WITH ME AS LONG AS I-
HE'S JUST NOT GOING TO **LEAVE**...

HERE IT COMES. THE PRESENT IS ABOUT TO COME INTO FOCUS...

I'LL BET THEY'RE ALL WAITING TO HEAR ABOUT MY TRIP...

HEY- WHERE ARE THEY? I THOUGHT THEY'D BE GATHERED AROUND...

OH. COMPANY.
"HE WHO NEEDS THE MOST HELP RESISTETH THE HARDEST."
OPEN UP YOUR LIFE TO US!
LEGGO MY **WALLET**!

RATLIFF- I'M GLAD YOU'RE BACK. NOW DO ME A FAVOR.
WHAT'S THAT?
...PUT ON YOUR SCRUFFIEST DUDS, SNEAK AROUND FRONT, AND START WRITING ON THIS.
CHECK.
©87 Sam Hurt NEW STREAM COMICS

WELL, I'M BACK FROM THE- **HEY, LOOK** IT'S A POOR PERSON WRITING A CHECK FOR HIS LAST FEW DOLLARS...

...RUNNING SHOES! -I SHOULD'VE TOLD HIM TO WEAR **RUNNING SHOES**...
ZZZIP

EYEBEAM

CAN I HELP YOU?
OH, **NO**! NOT **AGAIN**!
WHAT?
I NEED A GIFT FOR THE SPORTS LOVING MAN IN MY LIFE...

EVERY YEAR, "SPORTS ILLUMINATED" MAKES A 15-MINUTE COMMERCIAL AND SHOWS IT ABOUT 5 TIMES AN HOUR THROUGHOUT THE HOLIDAYS.
...PLUS, YOU GET THE SWIMSUIT ISSUE...
OH, THEY'LL LOVE THAT!

IN THIS ONE, A DEPARTMENT STORE CLERK TALKS A CROWD OF CUSTOMERS INTO ORDERING MAGAZINE SUBSCRIPTIONS INSTEAD OF SHOPPING IN HIS STORE.
WHAT WAS THAT NUMBER?
1-800...
©87 HURT

WE'LL BE BACK AFTER THIS...
AND THEY WONDER WHY THE SUICIDE RATE GOES UP ON HOLIDAYS...
1-800-WHAT?
CAN I HELP YOU?
I NEED A GIFT FOR THE SPORTS-LOVING MAN IN MY LIFE...

OH, **MAN**! I CAN'T **BELIEVE** THIS! THIS IS THE EIGHTH PAIR IN A **ROW**!
©87 Sam Hurt

NONE OF MY JEANS FIT ANYMORE! I MUST HAVE COOKED THEM TOO LONG IN THE DRYER...
ISN'T IT ALSO POSSIBLE YOU JUST OUTGREW THEM?

ALL OF THEM AT ONCE? WOULDN'T THAT BE A BIT OF A COINCIDENCE?

EYEBEAM

HEY, EYEBEAM. GUESS WHAT? I FOUND A JOB!
CONGRATULATIONS, RATLIFF! THAT'S ALWAYS GOOD NEWS.

HOLD ON. I'LL SHOW YOU MY UNIFORM...
LET'S HOPE THIS ONE LASTS LONGER THAN YOUR **LAST** FEW JOBS.
12-8

I GUESS IT'LL DEPEND ON HOW GOOD A JOB I DO.
MANNED OBSOLESCENCE.
©86 Sam Hurt

...AND A RAMBO DOLL, AND A G.I. JOE ACTION-WAR PACKAGE, AND A MASTERS OF THE UNIVERSE BATTLE GEAR!

JIMMY, IS THAT THE ONLY KIND OF TOY YOU LIKE?
WHAT DO YOU MEAN, SANTA?

WELL, THOSE ARE ALL TOYS WHERE YOU PRETEND TO BE FIGHTING...
AM I A BAD BOY?
12-9

NO, I DIDN'T MEAN TO- HEY, LET'S TALK ABOUT SOMETHING ELSE- WHAT DO YOU WANT TO BE WHEN YOU GROW UP?
PRESIDENT.

EYEBEAM

BOY- AFTER ABOUT SIX OR SEVEN HOURS, THAT STARTS TO FEEL LIKE **WORK**...

I CAN KEEP IT UP, THOUGH... I HAVE **PLENTY** OF HOLIDAY SPIRIT...
12-10

...ARGUABLY **TOO** MUCH.

SANTA, ALL I WANT THIS YEAR IS PEACE FOR ALL THE PEOPLE OF THE WORLD.
I DON'T BELIEVE MY EARS...

I'VE BEEN SITTING HERE FOR **WEEKS** LISTENING TO AN ENDLESS PROCESSION OF KIDS RECITE AN ANTHEM OF HUMAN GREED.

ONE EVEN HAD A TYPED LIST WITH 195 ITEMS ON IT! THEN, LIKE A BREATH OF FRESH AIR, YOU COME ALONG. I'M TRULY TOUCHED, UH...
... BILLY.
12-19

WELL, IT SEEMS TO BE WORKING SO FAR...
NOW **THINK**, BILLY- THERE MUST BE A FEW THINGS YOU'D LIKE FOR YOURSELF...

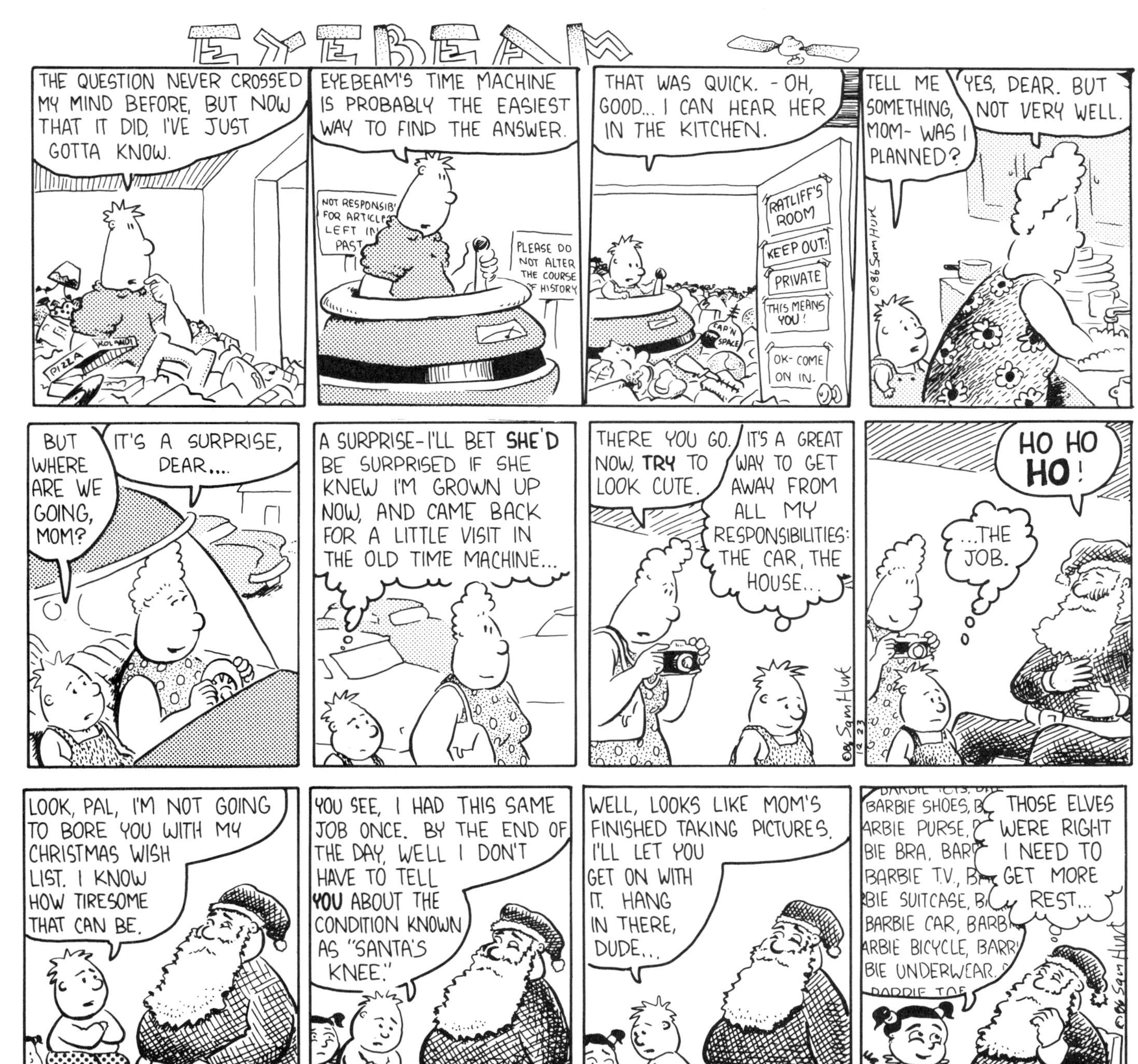
EYEBEAM
THE QUESTION NEVER CROSSED MY MIND BEFORE, BUT NOW THAT IT DID, I'VE JUST GOTTA KNOW.
PIZZA
EYEBEAM'S TIME MACHINE IS PROBABLY THE EASIEST WAY TO FIND THE ANSWER.
NOT RESPONSIB FOR ARTICLE LEFT IN PAST
PLEASE DO NOT ALTER THE COURSE OF HISTORY
THAT WAS QUICK. - OH, GOOD... I CAN HEAR HER IN THE KITCHEN.
RATLIFF'S ROOM
KEEP OUT!
PRIVATE
THIS MEANS YOU!
OK- COME ON IN.
CAP'N SPACE
TELL ME SOMETHING, MOM- WAS I PLANNED?
YES, DEAR. BUT NOT VERY WELL.
© 86 Sam Hurt
BUT WHERE ARE WE GOING, MOM?
IT'S A SURPRISE, DEAR....
A SURPRISE - I'LL BET SHE'D BE SURPRISED IF SHE KNEW I'M GROWN UP NOW, AND CAME BACK FOR A LITTLE VISIT IN THE OLD TIME MACHINE...
THERE YOU GO. NOW, TRY TO LOOK CUTE.
IT'S A GREAT WAY TO GET AWAY FROM ALL MY RESPONSIBILITIES: THE CAR, THE HOUSE...
©86 Sam Hurt 12-23
HO HO HO!
...THE JOB.
LOOK, PAL, I'M NOT GOING TO BORE YOU WITH MY CHRISTMAS WISH LIST. I KNOW HOW TIRESOME THAT CAN BE.
YOU SEE, I HAD THIS SAME JOB ONCE. BY THE END OF THE DAY, WELL I DON'T HAVE TO TELL YOU ABOUT THE CONDITION KNOWN AS "SANTA'S KNEE."
WELL, LOOKS LIKE MOM'S FINISHED TAKING PICTURES. I'LL LET YOU GET ON WITH IT. HANG IN THERE, DUDE...
BARBIE SHOES, BARBIE PURSE, BIE BRA, BARBIE T.V., BIE SUITCASE, BARBIE CAR, ARBIE BICYCLE, BIE UNDERWEAR.
THOSE ELVES WERE RIGHT I NEED TO GET MORE REST...
©86 Sam Hurt

BOY, A TIME-MACHINE CHRISTMAS IS QUITE AN EXPERIENCE. SEEING ALL THESE TOYS FOR THE FIRST TIME, AGAIN. **THIS** ONE LASTED FOREVER, THEN I LOST IT.
SPACE COWBOY

I STILL HAVE THIS ONE AROUND SOMEWHERE... BUT LOOK HOW BIG AND SHINY IT USED TO BE...
SPACE COWBOY

NOW, THIS ONE IS KIND OF A PUZZLER... I DON'T SEEM TO REMEMBER IT AT ALL... WELL, MAYBE JUST A FAINT-
SPACE COWBOY
12-25

...OH YEAH.
SPROING
SPACE COWBOY
©86 Sam Hurt

WELL, I GUESS I'LL HEAD BACK FORWARD IN TIME...
THE PRESENT. IT'S NOT MUCH, BUT I CALL IT HOME.
HEY- WHERE THE HECK **WERE** YOU?

IT'S VERY ANNOYING WHEN YOU CAN'T USE SOMETHING THAT **BELONGS** TO YOU BECAUSE SOMEONE ELSE IS ALWAYS **BORROWING** IT!
12-29

BUT, I RETURNED TO A POINT IN TIME ONLY 15 SECONDS LATER THAN WHEN I LEFT...
-AND YOU COULDN'T **PHONE** TO LET ME KNOW YOUR PLANS?
©86 Sam Hurt

ONE MOMENT. I'LL CHECK.

©88 Sam Hurt
Z Z Z

I'M SORRY. SHE'S CURRENTLY SNOOZATIONAL. CAN I TAKE A MESSAGE?
3-12

OH, BOY! WHAT A NAP! I WAS OUT COLD! DID I MISS ANY CALLS?
YES - YOU'VE BEEN SELECTED TO PARTICIPATE IN A UNIQUE MARKETING PROGRAM. FOR ONLY $30, YOU CAN RECEIVE A PACKAGE OF COUPONS WORTH OVER $400

OH, BOY LOOK AT THAT ASHEN COUNTENANCE.

A GRIM LOOK OF BETRAYAL AND DISILLUSIONMENT... WHAT'S THE **MATTER**, RATLIFF?

I WAS LAID OFF. I'M NOT GOING TO BE SANTA ANYMORE.
OH, GEE... I'M SORRY.
12-30

YOU'RE NOT GOING TO **BEIEVE** THE FLIMSY EXCUSE THEY GAVE ME.
DON'T TELL ME THEY TRIED THAT OLD SCAM ABOUT THE TIME OF YEAR!
© 86 Sam Hurt

RATLIFF, I KNOW YOU'RE UPSET ABOUT LOSING YOUR SANTA JOB, BUT JUST **LOOK** AT YOURSELF...

...YOU WEAR THAT BATHROBE ALL DAY-YOU DRAG THE T.V. EVERYWHERE YOU GO.

OK, SO YOU'VE HAD A SETBACK. IT'S TIME TO PULL YOURSELF TOGETHER AND SAY "WHAT'S NEXT?"
12-31

I'VE DECIDED TO DEVOTE MY LIFE TO MOPING.
WELL, AS LONG AS YOU HAVE A PURPOSE.
©86 Sam Hurt

I'M SORRY I GOT SO RIDICULOUSLY UPSET ABOUT LOSING MY JOB, EYEBEAM.
I KNOW YOU REALLY HAD HIGH HOPES FOR THAT JOB, RATLIFF...

HOPE IS A FLAMING TORCH-IF IT BURNS **TOO** BRIGHTLY, YOU CAN BE CONSUMED IN IT, THEN INCINERATED BY DISAPPOINTMENT.
AND YET, IT'S IMPORTANT NEVER TO LET IT GO COMPLETELY OUT.
1-2 ©87 Sam Hurt

...HOPE IS A PILOT LIGHT.
THAT'S ONE REVELATION THAT BELONGS ON THE BACK BURNER.

YOUR HONOR, THE DEFENSE OBJECTS TO THIS EXHIBIT. WE FEEL THAT PLACING IT INTO EVIDENCE COULD ONLY SERVE TO PREJUDICE THE JURY...

I NEED A LAWYER! I WAS THE VICTIM OF GROSS NEGLIGENCE! - OH, WHY MINCE WORDS?... IT WAS **WILLFUL** MISCONDUCT!

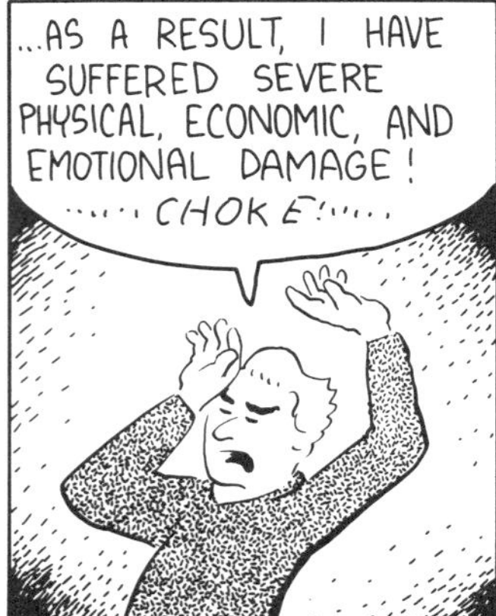
...AS A RESULT, I HAVE SUFFERED SEVERE PHYSICAL, ECONOMIC, AND EMOTIONAL DAMAGE! ......CHOKE!.....

I'M AN EMPTY SHELL OF MY FORMER SELF... I DON'T KNOW HOW I CAN GO ON... EVERYBODY JUST LEAVE ME ALONE!!

WELL, WHAT DO YOU THINK? DO I HAVE A FUTURE IN LITIGATION?
AUDITIONS ARE THURSDAY, KID...

SO, BILLY AND I WERE BEST BUDDIES IN THE THIRD AND FOURTH GRADE, BUT EVER SINCE HE GOT INTO CUB SCOUTS, HE ONLY PLAYS WITH JERRY CUSSLER.

KID, I CAN'T EVEN TELL YOU WHY, BUT YOU DON'T HAVE A "PALIMONY" SUIT HERE.

MY CLIENT, LIKE YOU AND ME, IS A HUMAN BEING. LIKE YOU AND ME, HE'S MADE MISTAKES ALONG THE WAY.

AND IN THE GRAND SCHEME, IT'S CLEAR THAT MISTAKES ARE PART OF A PROCESS IN WHICH WE CHANGE, WE GROW, WE IMPROVE OURSELVES WE... WE...

WE... WE... UH...

OK. APPARENTLY, MY CLIENT IS SOME SORT OF SLIME-MOLD. BUT LIKE YOU AND ME, HE DESERVES HIS DAY IN COURT...

HEY, EYEBEAM- DO YOU EVER FEEL LIKE YOU'RE IN A RUT THAT'S GETTING SO DEEP YOU CAN'T SEE OVER THE SIDES ANY MORE?

WHAT DO YOU MEAN, VERNON?

THERE'S NO VARIETY IN OUR ROUTINE- LIFE HAS BECOME SO UNIFORM THAT THERE ARE NO SEAMS ANYMORE- JUST ONE LONG, CONTINUOUS-
UH OH- BREAK'S OVER. LET'S CONTINUE THIS CONVERSATION AFTER WORK...
MAXWELL HOUSE

ARE WE DOING OK HERE?
OK- WHERE WERE WE?

WHAT ARE WE HERE TO DECIDE TODAY? HOW DID WE COME TO SIT IN JUDGMENT OVER OTHER PEOPLE'S DISPUTES? COULD A SYSTEM LIKE THIS EXIST IN ANY OTHER COUNTRY? AM I ANY DIFFERENT FROM YOU JUST BECAUSE I HAVE LITTLE DOTS PRINTED ON MY FACE? HOW WILL FUTURE GENERATIONS LOOK UPON WHAT WE DECIDE HERE TODAY?

PSSSST....

2-19

EYEBEAM

©87 Sam Hurt

EYEBEAM LITE
THIS PARTY HAS EVERYTHING, BUT IT'S JUST NOT **HAPPENING.**
BEEP BEEP
HEY, LOOK WHO'S HERE! THE PARTY WILL COOK NOW!
©87 Sam Hurt
IT'S SPUDS McFRENZY - THE PARTY POTATO!

HE'S SO HOT!
HE'S SO COOL!
CALL ME, SPUDS!
HE'S ONE HAPPENING VEGETABLE!

THERE'S A WEIRD TREND IN ADVERTISING. I DON'T THINK I LIKE WHERE IT'S GOING...
WHAT DO YOU MEAN?
OH... SPUDS OH...
SPUDS

YOU KNOW, MOLENE, YOU AND I COULD END UP AS ONE OF THOSE FAMOUS LEGAL TEAMS.
YEAH, I CAN SEE US NOW, MAKING COMMERCIALS: "HAVE YOU BEEN INJURED IN AN ACCIDENT BY SOMEONE WITH A LOT OF MONEY OR INSURANCE? CALL MOLENE AND VERNON."
©88 Sam Hurt
I HAD IN MIND SOMETHING A LITTLE MORE HIGH-POWERED.
SENATOR SCRUDE - DID YOU REALLY SELL IRANIAN DRUGS TO THE CONTRAS?
I DON'T KNOW. ASK MY LAWYERS.
HE'S INNOCENT. BACK OFF.
MEDIA JACKALS!
5
2-27
WHEW! UNBRIDLED AMBITION CAN BE MIGHTY REFRESHING!
GOES BETTER WITH COFFEE THAN THOSE LITTLE ROLLS WE USUALLY HAVE...

VERNON, I HAVE A BAD FEELING ABOUT THIS CASE. HAVE YOU SEEN OUR OPPOSING COUNSEL?
MOLENE, WE'VE BEEN UP AGAINST TITAN & MAGNUM! WE'VE DONE BATTLE WITH SALIVA and SLOTH. WE'VE RUN THE GAMUT.
©88 Sam Hurt

RIGHT. WE CAN HANDLE ANYTHING NOW.
...IT'S ONLY A LAWSUIT. I'M SURE, NO MATTER WHO IT IS, I'M SURE WE CAN.

3-10

WE'RE THE LAWYERS FOR THE OTHER SIDE ON THIS WEEK'S "L.A. LAW"...
LET'S SLINK OUT AND SETTLE DURING THE FIRST COMMERCIAL.

HAVE YOU BEEN HURT OR INJURED IN AN ACCIDENT?
SORT OF. I'M DRIVING THE COMPANY TRUCK, DOING SEVENTY. A TIRE BLOWS! I BARELY MISS THAT RETAINING WALL.

AT SALIVA A
SLOTH. WE'R
TOUGH, SMA
LAWYERS W
KNOW HOW
TO GO AFT
THE MONEY YOU
HAVE COMIN
EVER SINCE, I HAVEN'T FELT LIKE DOING ANYTHING... OTHERWISE, I'D PROBABLY BE PRESIDENT BY NOW.
©87 Sam Hurt

CALL NOW, BEFORE IT'S TOO LATE FOR US TO PROTECT YOUR RIGHTS...
HE'S RIGHT! -TIME FOR ACTION. WHERE'S THAT PHONE?

WE ALSO SPECIALIZE IN CONSEQUENTIAL DAMAGES...
UH... GOOD.

EYEBEAM
OK- QUIET EVERYBODY. IT'S ABOUT TO START. I DECIDED IT'S TIME FOR THE FIRM TO MOVE WITH THE TIMES...
"BARNABY JONES" WILL RETURN AFTER THIS...
GEE- I'VE BEEN HURT OR INJURED IN AN ACCIDENT- WHAT SHOULD I DO?
AS A PROFESSIONAL, I'D SAY YOU NEED A LAWYER. AND EVERYBODY KNOWS WHO THE BEST IS...
FIRM NAME HERE
SMACK
SMACK
SMACK
IT'S TIMES LIKE THIS I WISH I HAD A FOREHEAD...
EYEBEAM

EYEBEAM
OBJECTION, ADMISSION OF THIS EVIDENCE WOULD BE IMPROPER.
SUSTAINED. THE JURY IS INSTRUCTED TO DISREGARD THE EXHIBIT.
DANG!
EYEBEAM

EYEBEAM
SO, YOU'RE SAYING THAT-
THERE IT GOES AGAIN-THE CAR OF MY **DREAMS**!
YOU MEAN THAT ONE?
YEAH!...I'D **KILL** FOR THAT CAR!
SO YOU REALLY LIKE IT, HUH?
OH, YAS!...I COULD FIND TRUE PEACE WITH A CAR LIKE THAT-INNER HARMONY-PERSONAL FULFILLMENT...
I'M NOT SURE LUST BECOMES YOU, RATLIFF...
DRIVE ME, BABY- **DRIVE ME**!

EYEBEAM
NATURAL LAWS
ONE WAY
TWO WRONGS DON'T MAKE A RIGHT...
...BUT THREE RIGHTS **DO** MAKE A LEFT...

HEY, IM4U- WHAT EVER HAPPENED TO YOUR WIFE, SYNTHEA?
SYNTHEA AND I ARE SPLITSVILLE, EYEBEAM...
©'87 Sam Hurt

OH. I'M SORRY TO HEAR THAT...
SHE'S IMPOSSIBLE. SHE THINKS THAT JUST BECAUSE I DESIGNED AND BUILT HER, I WANT TO CONTROL HER LIFE...

TYPICAL.
IT'S HARD TO WORK THINGS OUT WHEN YOU'RE DEALING WITH AN ATTITUDE PROBLEM LIKE THAT...

PLUS, I'LL BET SHE CAUGHT YOU FOOLING AROUND WITH SOME GADGET OR APPLIANCE.
IT'S NOT FAIR! THAT PARKING METER AND I WERE JUST GOOD FRIENDS!

OH, NO! STOP THAT, GASKET! WHY DO YOU ALWAYS HAVE TO EMBARRASS ME LIKE THIS..?
©'87 Sam Hurt

DOGS HAVE A DISGUSTING WAY OF SNIFFING AT THE LEAST APPROPRIATE PLACE THEY CAN FIND...
NEW STREAM COMICS

ALL RIGHT, GASKET - THAT'S ENOUGH. LET'S GO...
SNIFF SNIFF

I NEVER NOTICED YOU HAD A DOG, IM4U...
YOU MEAN OLD GASKET? YEAH... HE'S A GOOD OLD DOG, ALL RIGHT...

...HE'S FAITHFUL, OBEDIENT...
©'87 Sam H.

...AND HE'S A PRETTY DARN GOOD MOUSER, TOO...
ARF..

EYEBEAM
YOU KNOW, EYEBEAM, I RECENTLY MANAGED TO MAKE IT BY MY OLD SCHOOL REUNION.
SCHOOL ? ROBOTS GO TO SCHOOL ?
©87 Sam Hurt

YES. MUCH OF OUR KNOWLEDGE IS PROGRAMMED-IN, BUT THE MORE SUBTLE THINGS, LIKE FASHION SENSE, MUST BE LEARNED.
RIGHT. SO HOW WAS THE REUNION?

IT WAS KIND OF EERIE, EYEBEAM. NO ONE SEEMED TO HAVE CHANGED A BIT.
GOOD OLD SOLID STATE U.

EYEBEAM
SURROGATE PARENTING CENTER
©87 Sam Hurt

SO YOU AND SYNTHEA ARE SPLITSVILLE, YOU SAY.
IRRECONCILABLE DIFFERENCES. SHE SAYS MEGAHERTZ I SAY KILOVOLTS.
©87 Sam Hurt

I DON'T KNOW WHAT TO SAY. I'M SORRY, IM4U.
DON'T SWEAT IT. IT'S ANTIFREEZE UNDER THE BRIDGE, NOW. BUT I WOULD LIKE TO BORROW YOUR WORKSHOP AND ANY SCRAP METAL YOU MIGHT HAVE LYING AROUND.

ROUGH PROPERTY SETTLEMENT?
YOU COULD SAY THAT.

I'M SURPRISED I NEVER HEARD FROM YOU DURING YOUR DIVORCE FROM SYNTHEA.
I CHOSE TO REPRESENT MYSELF, EYEBEAM.

OH. IM4U. THAT WAS A BIG MISTAKE.
SURE WAS. SHE GOT A REAL HIGH- POWERED LAWYER. THE GUY HAD ME FOR BREAKFAST...

ANYBODY I KNOW?
I DOUBT IT THIS GUY IS NEW...

PART MAN - PART ROBOT- BOARD CERTIFIED IN ALL SPECIALIZATIONS:
ROBO-LAWYER
WHIRRRRRR
WREEEEEE
I'VE ALREADY PREPARED A BRIEF ON THAT SUBJECT...
CLICK

SO YOUR EX-WIFE'S LAWYER WAS A POWERHOUSE, HUH?
OH, HE HAD THE JUDGE EATING OUT OF HIS HAND!
SO YOU ADMIT YOU ENTERED INTO A SHAMELESS AFFAIR WITH A 1958 STUDEBAKER?
WELL, I'VE ALWAYS HAD THIS FANTASY ABOUT OLDER CARS. I'M SURE YOU'VE BEEN THERE.

YOUR HONOR, I'D ALSO LIKE THE RECORD TO SHOW THAT I TOOK GOOD CARE O-
FREEZE!

... I MEAN, "OBJECTION."
SUSTAINED... SUSTAINED!
THANKS. NOW I FORGOT WHAT I WAS GOING TO SAY...

EYEBEAM
I DON'T MIND DRIVING AN OLD HEAP LIKE THIS... IT'S ALL IN YOUR ATTITUDE
sam Hurt
©87
I MEAN, THIS CAR HAS **CHARACTER**... IT HAS **CLASS** -AND THE MORE YOUR CAR HAS, THE MORE **YOU** HAVE...

...GENERALLY SPEAKING...

ON THE GOOOOOOD SHIP...
LOLLEEPOP...
SHIRLEY

AFTER YOU'VE SEEN THESE PICTURES, I THINK YOU'LL AGREE THAT WE WOULDN'T WANT THEM TO FALL INTO THE WRONG HANDS...
BY THE WAY, I HAVE SOME BACKUP COPIES...
THE ANTI SHIRLEY

I LIKE WHAT YOU'VE DONE TO YOUR YARD, RATLIFF - SUCH A NATURAL EFFECT...
THANKS, BUT YOU'D BETTER NOT STAND IN THAT TALL GRASS...

OH. WHAT'S THE PROBLEM? PARASITES?
SORT OF...

OW OW OW HEY!
DOWN, GIRL - DOWN! WE CAN PLAY "LAWN PIRANHA" LATER...

AUNT SALLY, WOULD YOU READ ME A BEDTIME STORY?
OK. DO YOU HAVE IT WITH YOU?

YEAH. HERE IT IS.
WHAT IS IT? GOLDILOCKS? LITTLE RED RIDING HOOD?

"TRAILS IN BLOOD - FAMOUS SERIAL MURDER CASES"?
YEAH. I'VE HEARD IT BEFORE, BUT GO AHEAD...

LOOK AT THIS - SOMEBODY'S OLD COWBOY OUTFIT...

KIND OF MAKES YOU THINK. WHAT WOULD IT BE LIKE, HAVING TO DEPEND ON PRIMITIVE TOOLS LIKE THESE FOR POWER? YES, LIFE WOULD SURE BE DIFFERENT IF I WEREN'T QUEEN OF THE UNIVERSE...
Sam Hurt '87

KIDS! THEY'RE ALWAYS PLAYING "WHAT IF"...
WHAT IF I WERE MERELY HUMAN, LIKE OTHER PEOPLE ?...

THROUGHOUT HISTORY, MAN HAS ENGAGED IN A VERY SPECIAL NOCTURNAL RITUAL WITH HIS REFRIGERATOR.
AT LAST-AFTER YEARS OF PLOTTING AND SCHEMING, THE MALTESE PIG IS ACTUALLY WITHIN HER GRASP...
SHE CHERISHES THE TOUCH OF ITS ALABASTER SMOOTHNESS
SHE CREEPS THROUGH THE INKY BLACKNESS LIKE A CAT, WHEN SUDDENLY-

UNCLE RATLIFF, WOULD YOU READ ME A BEDTIME STORY?
WHY, IT WOULD BE A PRIVILEGE TO TAKE PART IN THAT TIME-HONORED TRADITION, PEACHES.
PAT PAT
©87 Sam Hurt

OH. YOU BROUGHT YOUR BOOK WITH YOU. DOES IT HAVE PICTURES?
NO, BUT IT LOOKS PRETTY GOOD ANYWAY.

"NURSES ON SPEED- A HORRIFYING INSIDE ACCOUNT OF THE FREDVILLE MUTILATIONS"!?
"DICK AND JANE" JUST DON'T GRAB ME, OK?

EYEBEAM

HIGH ABOVE THE VELDT SOARS A BLACK SILHOUETTE...

FROM HORIZON TO HORIZON, THERE SEEMS TO BE ONLY PARCHED GRASS-LAND, BUT THE HAWK'S KEEN EYE SPOTS A MOVING SHADOW... SHE TURNS, PIVOTS IN THE WIND, AND...
DIVES

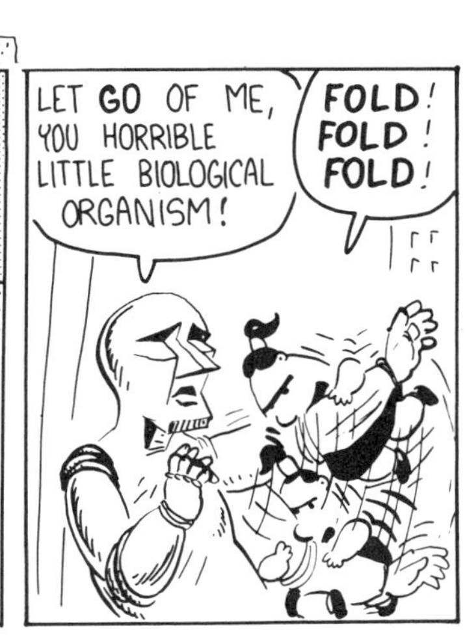

LET GO OF ME, YOU HORRIBLE LITTLE BIOLOGICAL ORGANISM!
FOLD! FOLD! FOLD!

WHY DO YOU PERSECUTE ME, LITTLE GIRL? I HAVE **ENOUGH** PROBLEMS!
I **KNOW** YOU'RE A ROBOT- NOW, **FOLD**!

THATS THE ONLY PROBLEM WITH THIS PLANET- ALL THE CHILDREN SEEM TO THINK ROBOTS ARE MADE TO TRANSFORM INTO SOME KIND OF TOY...
DON'T YOU KNOW **ANYTHING**? DON'T YOU EVEN WATCH TV?

LATER:
EXPLAIN TO HER THAT FREEDOM IS FOR ALL BEINGS; ARTIFICIAL **AND** ORGANIC!
MAKE HIM **FOLD**, UNCLE EYEBEAM.
I MUST BE A **MAGNET** FOR THIS KIND OF THING...

NOW PEACHES, ONLY **TOY** ROBOTS FOLD. IM4U IS REAL.
YEAH- I'M MADE FOR **OTHER** USES.
I DEMAND SATISFACTION. I WANT TO SEE HIM **FOLD**.

THAT'S THE WAY THE REAL WORLD **IS**, PEACHES- YOU CAN'T HAVE EVERYTHING YOU WANT...
HE'S RIGHT. YOU'RE JUST GOING TO HAVE TO **LIVE** WITH IT...
I'LL STAND ON MY HEAD UNTIL MY FACE TURNS PURPLE...

I GUESS **YOU** REALIZE YOU COULD MAKE LIFE A LOT EASIER FOR ALL OF US...
DARNIT, IT'S A MATTER OF PRINCIPLE NOW.

CAN I HELP YOU?
I DON'T KNOW. MAYBE. YOU SEE, I KNOW THIS LITTLE GIRL WHO, FOR SOME REASON, HAS AN INTENSE NEED TO SEE A ROBOT FOLD INTO SOME OTHER TOY.
TOYS "**2**" BUY
TRANSFOR

IT SO HAPPENS I HAVE JUST THE THING FOR HER...
YOU **DO**? WHAT A COINCIDENCE...
TOYS "**4**" BRATS
TRANSFOR

IT'S NO COINCIDENCE! MAKING KIDS HAPPY IS OUR **BUSINESS**!
HELLO.. LET'S PLAY... BANG, YOU'RE DEAD...
DOLLS "**P**" TOO

HEY, PEACHES-
LOOK WHAT WE
GOT FOR YOU-
A TOY ROBOT!
...AND WAIT TILL
YOU SEE WHAT
IT DOES...

SEE? -IT
FOLDED UP!
IT TRANSFORMED!
IT'S A TANK
NOW...HOW DO
YOU LIKE THAT?
SNAP
FLIP
CLICK

E Y E B E A M

HEY- LOOKS LIKE IT WORKED!
SHE CERTAINLY **SEEMS** SATISFIED.

IT'S AN ALMOST ZEN-LIKE SERENITY.
LOOKS LIKE SHE'S FOUND THAT TRANQUILITY MOST OF US SPEND A LIFETIME SEARCHING FOR..

THAT PROVES IT. WHEN YOU AND I PUT OUR MINDS TOGETHER, WE GET RESULTS...
BUT OF COURSE!
THIS MEANS I'LL GET TO SEE THE **BIG** ONE FOLD...
©87 Sam Hurt

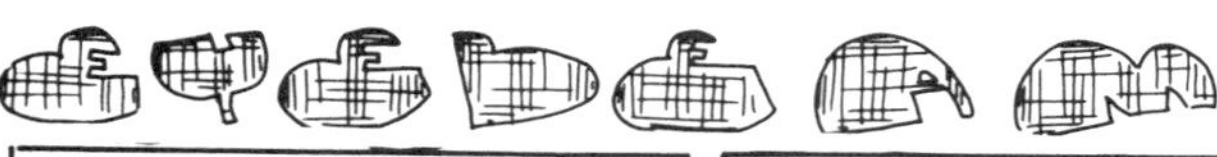

HELLO. LETS PLAY... LOOK- I'M A ROBOT...
Sam Hurt ©87

NOW I'M A TANK... **BANG BANG**!

TECHNOLOGY HAS TRULY CHANGED OUR LIVES...
YEAH... EVEN TOYS WILL NEVER BE THE SAME...
TELL YOUR PARENTS ABOUT MY FINE NEW LINE OF ACCESSORIES...

EYEBEAM
I'VE ALWAYS WANTED ONE OF THESE...
HELLO... LET'S PLAY... BANG BANG!
©87 Sam Hurt NEW STREAM COMICS
I PLEADED. I BEGGED. I TRIED LIES. I TRIED THREATS.
TELL YOUR PARENTS ABOUT MY FINE LINE OF ACCESSORIES.
NOW I'VE GOT IT, AND I'M LUCKY TO BE HAVING SO MUCH FUN...
WE'RE SAFE, EDUCATIONAL, AND DURABLE...
...OTHERWISE, I'D BE BORED NUMB...
HELLO... LET'S PLAY... BANG BANG!

HI, IM4U. HAS PEACHES TRIED TO FOLD YOU LATELY?
NO. EVER SINCE YOU GAVE HER THAT DECOY TOY ROBOT, SHE'S BEEN OFF MY CASE, EYEBEAM.

WELL, AT THE RISK OF BRAGGING, I FEEL I DID A PRETTY GOOD JOB OF FIGURING OUT WHAT MAKES THE LITTLE CHERUB TICK...
PLUS, YOU PROVIDED A MUCH HEALTHIER OUTLET FOR ALL THAT YOUTHFUL ENERGY OF HERS...

THANKS TO HIS ATONOMIC NERVOUS SYSTEM, G.I. JOE FIGHTS BRAVELY ON, BUT HIS MARKSMANSHIP CONTINUES TO SUFFER.
zzzzZAP!
BLAM!! BLAM!!

COME ALONG, MISS MUFFINS. YOU'RE INVITED TO A TEA PARTY...
©87 Sam Hurt
NEW STREAM COMICS

NOW, WHOEVER MADE THE SEATING ARRANGEMENT PUT YOU RIGHT ACROSS FROM SNUFTOR, EVIL ROBOT ASSASSIN. HERE, LET ME POUR...
SHOES

ZAP
THUD

POOR MISS MUFFINS! IF ONLY SHE'D KNOWN THAT IN CERTAIN SITUATIONS, YOU SIMPLY **DON'T** PUT YOUR ELBOWS ON THE TABLE...
RIP

BO-BO THE BEAR IS WALKING THROUGH THE WOODS WITHOUT A CARE IN THE WORLD...
©87 Sam Hurt
BARBIE FOREST

HE CHUCKLES TO HIMSELF, THINKING BACK ON A TIME WHEN HE STOLE PUDDING FROM A LITTLE GIRL. AS HE ROUNDS A BEND IN THE PATH, THE CHUCKLE DIES ABRUPTLY IN HIS THROAT.
NEW STREAM COMICS

HIS STOMACH TIGHTENS. HE SEARCHES HIS MEMORY FRANTICALLY- WHAT HAD THE LITTLE GIRL SAID? ...THAT SOMEDAY HE'D **PAY** FOR THE PUDDING?

DID YOU HEAR SOMETHING, EYEBEAM?
THERE ARE SOME THINGS WE'RE BETTER OFF NOT KNOWING ABOUT, SALLY...

OH, **MY**!

HEY, EYEBEAM- COME LOOK AT PEACHES' ROOM. IT'S ALL-
I KNOW. YOU SEE, SHE WAS ALWAYS TRYING TO FOLD IM4U, SO WE BOUGHT HER A TOY ROBOT THAT'S **MADE** TO FOLD. ONLY ONE PROBLEM-
©87 SAM HURT

...IT WASTED ALL HER OTHER TOYS...
IT TOOK 'EM OUT ONE AT A TIME...
NEW STREAM COMICS

IT'S NOT **FAIR**! THEY WERE INNOCENT LITTLE **CHILDREN'S** TOYS!
HEY, IT'S A FIERCELY COMPETITIVE MARKET...

EYEBEAM

SNUFTOR, EVIL ROBOT ASSASSIN, SURVEYS THE PANORAMA OF DEVASTATION HE HAS CREATED...

A GLOATING SMIRK SEEMS TO PLAY ACROSS HIS CRUELLY METALLIC FEATURES...
©87 Sam Hurt

HIS PLAN FOR TURNING THE WHOLE UNIVERSE INTO A GRISLY DEATH-PIT IS GOING WELL. EVERY DETAIL IS UNDER HIS CONTROL.

WELL... **ALMOST** EVERY DETAIL...

EYEBEAM

THE EVIL ROBOT, SNUFTOR IS BUSY BEING DOWNRIGHT NASTY...

UNTIL THE QUEEN OF THE UNIVERSE BOLDLY INTERRUPTS...
HEY, YOU!
©87 Sam Hurt

THE TWO MIGHTY TITANS FACE OFF. THIS BATTLE WILL DETERMINE THE FATE OF THE PLANET. WHO WILL TRIUMPH? ONLY ONE THING IS CERTAIN...

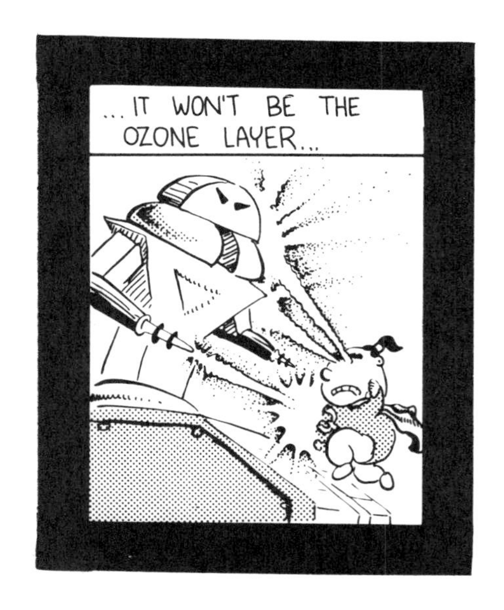
...IT WON'T BE THE OZONE LAYER...

HUTGN!

CRASH

DARNIT, PEACHES- YOU'RE GOING TO HAVE TO START TAKING BETTER CARE OF YOUR TOYS!
IF ONLY HE KNEW...

EYEBEAM
DON'T YOU JUST **HATE** CARRYING THE TRAY OF CACTUS AROUND AT A PARTY? WHY DO **I** ALWAYS GET STUCK WITH THIS JOB?
I MEAN, YOU CAN'T RELAX AND ENJOY YOURSELF BECAUSE YOU'RE CONSTANTLY WORRYING THAT-
©87 Sam Hurt
WHOOP!
EEK!
HEY, THIS IS GREAT! MAYBE MY PERSONALITY **DOES** HAVE A DARK, SINISTER UNDERSIDE!

EYEBEAM
HELLO. BUREAU OF BUREAUCRATIC INFORMATION...
YES- I'M CALLING FOR INFORMATION ON YOUR REDUNDANCY MANAGEMENT PROGRAM...
©87 Sam Hurt
ONE MOMENT...
CLICK...
CLICK ...HELLO, MAY I HELP YOU?
YES. I NEED TO TALK TO SOMEONE ABOUT YOUR REDUNDANCY MANAGEMENT PROGRAM...
I'LL TRANSFER YOU... ...YES?
YEAH...UH, I'M CALLING ABOUT...
YES. I CAN MAIL YOU THAT INFORMATION. WHAT'S YOUR ADDRESS?
FINALLY!... ONE MOMENT, I'LL TRANSFER YOU...

EYEBEAM
©87 Sam Hurt
KER-
SPLUNK
THAT'S PECULIAR- I CAN'T SEEM TO FIND ANYTHING AT ALL ABOUT LIQUID CACTUS...
FREUD
JUNG
DR RUTH

©87 HURT

YOU'RE AT HOME. ALL ALONE. BUT YOU CAN'T SHAKE OFF AN UNEASY FEELING - YOU SENSE THE PRESENCE OF AN UNWELCOME VISITOR...
©87 Sam Hurt

THE NORMAL CREAKS AND GROANS OF AN EMPTY HOUSE SEEM TO HAVE A STRANGELY OMINOUS TONE.

SUDDENLY, A CHILLING REALIZATION GRIPS YOU: IT IS ALREADY TOO LATE.

SNUFTOR II
THE NIGHT HE GOT NEW BATTERIES
COMING SOON TO A PLAYROOM NEAR YOU.

MOBY, THE MAFIA DUCK, IS WADDLING THROUGH AN ABANDONED ARMY SURPLUS STORE, WAITING TO MEET HIS "CONNECTION"...
BUT SOMETHING DOESN'T SEEM QUITE RIGHT. "THEY WOULDN'T **DARE** DOUBLE-CROSS **ME**!", HE THINKS...
BUT HE'S WRONG.
SPROING
OH, DON'T TELL ME YOU FIXED THAT DARNED ROBOT! NOW IT'LL DESTROY THE REST OF YOUR TOY COLLECTION!
A MEDDLESOME UNCLE STUMBLES UPON THE SCENE. HE NOW KNOWS TOO MUCH...
NO! I DIDN'T SEE A **THING**!

I'M SORRY, UNCLE RATLIFF, BUT YOU KNOW TOO MUCH...
NO! I SAW **NOTHING**! I WAS JUST STRAIGHTENING UP - YOU KNOW HOW WE GROWNUPS ARE...
THIS IS GOING TO HURT ME MORE THAN IT HURTS YOU- **SICK 'EM**, SNUFTOR!
SPEAKING OF STRAIGHTENING UP, I'D BETTER GET BACK TO IT...
PREPARE TO DIE, EARTHLING!
I CHALK THIS UP TO TOO MUCH VIOLENCE ON TELEVISION...

EYEBEAM

THE GIANT ROBOT OF DEATH CLOSES IN...
NO... NO!

NO!... DON'T SHOOT!
©87 Sam Hurt

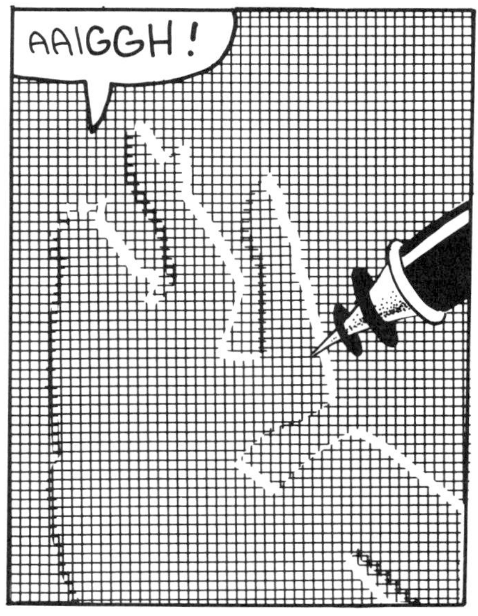

AAIGGH!

THANK GOODNESS FOR THAT FINE LINE BETWEEN FANTASY AND REALITY. OTHERWISE, I'D BE SPLATTERED ALL OVER THE FOURTH DIMENSION!
YECCCCCH. WHAT A MESS!

HEY, EYEBEAM- I GOT A JOB IN THE PRODUCT GLORIFICATION INDUSTRY!
YOU MEAN YOU'LL BE MAKING COMMERCIALS AGAIN?

THIS TIME IT'LL BE DIFFERENT. I'LL BE PROMOTING SOMETHING I REALLY **BELIEVE** IN.
OH, **NO**!

...A PRODUCT I'VE GROWN UP WITH; ONE MY WHOLE **FAMILY** TRUSTS! GUESS WHICH...
I THINK I ALREADY HAVE...

EVERYBODY COMPARES THEIR PRODUCT TO **OURS**... -EVER WONDER WHY?
BRAND
BRAND X
BRAND X detergent

BOY, LIFE IS REALLY DIFFERENT WHEN YOU'RE WORKING! YOU HAVE TO GET UP EARLY AND SPEND ALL DAY DRESSED.

...YOU COME HOME; YOU'RE TIRED; THE MESS YOU MADE IN THE MORNING GETTING READY IS EXACTLY THE WAY YOU LEFT IT...

WHAT THE..!..

IT'S AN ADJUSTMENT FOR THE PETS, TOO...
BRAND

RUMORS... RUMORS... RUMORS...
TIC

...I AM **SICK** AND **TIRED** OF HEARING THESE STUPID RUMORS THAT SOME COMPETITOR IS ATTEMPTING A HOSTILE TAKEOVER OF "THREE INITIAL COMPANY"!

I DON'T WANT TO HEAR ANY MORE ABOUT IT UNTIL THERE'S SOME TANGIBLE EVIDENCE...
TIC
BRAND X

IT'S GREAT BEING A BIG EXECUTIVE WITH "THREE INITIAL COMPANY"...
TIC
WONG
THUDCO

I GUESS THE PART I LIKE BEST IS KNOWING I'M WITH **THE** COMPANY- **THE** BIGGEST; **THE** BEST; **THE** ULTIMATE!
DON'T LOOK NOW, BUT THERE ARE A LOT OF **OTHER** COMPANIES OUT THERE...AND SOME OF THEM ARE MOVING FAST.

MAYBE SO, BUT THEY'LL NEVER TOUCH **US**...
TIC
BRAND X
WONG
THUDCO

WELL, HERE I AM IN MY NEW SHADES. I WONDER IF I LOOK COOL?

UH-OH.- THOSE GIRLS SEEM TO BE GIGGLING AT ME. DO MY GLASSES LOOK SILLY ON ME? WAS IT DORKY OF ME TO WEAR THEM OUT OF THE STORE?
THE SHADE STORE

THIS IS THE KIND OF THING THAT WREAKS HAVOC ON MY SELF-IMAGE...

IT USED TO MAKE ME SO PROUD TO BE PART OF A GRAND ENTERPRISE LIKE "THREE INITIAL COMPANY."
TIC
STANDING PROUDLY TALL

BUT NOW, I CAN'T BELIEVE I'M PART OF A- I DON'T **WANT** TO BE IN A- **ANYTHING** BUT A-
SAY IT, ROD! SAY THE WORDS. YOU HAVE TO WORK THROUGH THIS...
STANDING PROUDLY TALL

...WHOLLY OWNED SUBSIDIARY.
BRAND X
TIC

LOOK, EYEBEAM - THIS PHOTO REPRESENTS THE SPLENDOR THAT WAS ONCE THREE INITIAL COMPANY.
GEE... HOW AWE-INSPIRING.
TIC

BUT LOOK AT IT NOW. A HOSTILE TAKEOVER HAS ROBBED US OF OUR INDEPENDENCE!
BRAND X
TIC
THEY'VE TAKEN YOU UNDER THEIR WING...

NOW THE CORPORATE LEECHES **I** WORK FOR ARE UNDER A WHOLE NEW SET OF **THEIR** CORPORATE LEECHES. IT DOESN'T IMPROVE MY OPPORTUNITY FOR ADVANCEMENT...

YOU'RE A LAWYER, EYEBEAM! **HELP** ME! TELL ME WHAT TO DO! MAKE THINGS **RIGHT** AGAIN!
LET ME GET THIS STRAIGHT... YOU MEAN YOU'RE NOT EVEN A LEECH YET?

ACTUALLY, IT ALL STARTED WHEN MY COMPANY, TIC ATTEMPTED TO INFILTRATE THE BOARD OF DIRECTORS AT BRAND X...

BRAND X THEN PULLED SOME VERY SHADY, IF NOT QUESTIONABLE, MANEUVERS... AND NOW **WE'RE** THE WHOLLY OWNED SUBSIDIARY!
TIC
BRAND X

I'M OFFERING YOU A CHANCE TO UNTANGLE THIS MESS, EYEBEAM...
SORRY ROD, BUT A LAWYER CAN'T TAKE A CASE IF HE HAS A CONFLICT OF INTEREST...

HOW IS IT A CONFLICT OF INTEREST?
IT'S NOT THE KIND OF CONFLICT THAT HOLDS MY INTEREST...

TELL ME MORE ABOUT YOUR JOB, RATLIFF...
WELL, I'M SORT OF A CORPORATE SPOKESMAN FOR "BRAND X"...

HERE. MAYBE WE CAN CATCH ONE OF MY COMMERCIALS ON THE TUBE...
CLICK

BRAND X - THE PAPER TOWELS THAT ACTUALLY MAKE YOU **ENJOY** HOUSEHOLD SPILLS!
BRAND X

YOU'VE GOT TO **SEE** THIS, SALLY! YOU'LL BELIEVE A MAN CAN WIPE UP!
MORE SPECIAL EFFECTS.

TIME- SOME CONCEIVE OF IT AS THE FOURTH DIMENSION- THE ONE THAT HOLDS NOT ONLY LENGTH, WIDTH, AND HEIGHT, BUT MOVEMENT AND CHANGE AS WELL...
NOVEMBUARY

TIME- THE TRACK THAT CARRIES THE UNENDING FREIGHT TRAIN OF HISTORY. WE SIT HELPLESSLY AT THE CROSSING AND WATCH THE SMALL PART THAT PASSES DURING OUR LIFETIMES...

TIME- THE ELASTIC LINING IN THE WAISTBAND OF LIFE...
TIME MACHINE
TAMPER WITH DESTINY AT YOUR OWN RISK

...NOW AVAILABLE IN CONVENIENT SNACK-PACKS!

I ALWAYS ENJOY RETURNING TO MY PAST LIKE THIS...

IT'S A NICE OPPORTUNITY TO RELIVE THE SIMPLE PLEASURES OF CHILDHOOD..

IT'S ALSO A CHANCE TO EXPLORE MYSELF BY STUDYING FIRST-HAND THE ODD BUILDING BLOCKS OF MY FORMATIVE YEARS...
MIGHTY KONG

BEST OF ALL, THAT TAX RETURN DEADLINE IS ABOUT 20 YEARS AWAY...

HEY- WHAT IF, INSTEAD OF RETURNING TO THE PRESENT IN THE TIME MACHINE, I JUST USE NORMAL TIME AND RETURN BY GROWING UP ALL OVER AGAIN..?

WITH THE BENEFIT OF HINDSIGHT, I'D BE PREPARED FOR EVERY LITTLE THING THAT COMES ALONG. I COULD HANDLE IT ALL BETTER THAN I DID THE FIRST TIME AROUND...

I'D HAVE CONFIDENCE. I COULD CONTROL MY OWN DESTINY! WHO KNOWS **WHERE** IT MIGHT LEAD? I'LL HAVE TO GIVE THIS SERIOUS CONSIDERATION!

ARE YOU READY, RATLIFF? TIME TO GO TO THE DENTIST.
THEN AGAIN, IT MIGHT BE BEST NOT TO INTERFERE WITH THE COURSE OF HISTORY...

EYEBEAM
LOOK AT ME. I'M A ROBOT WITH A SPLIT PERSONALITY.
AREN'T WE ALL...

SO- HOW'S IT GOING?
GREAT!
TERRIBLE!
YES. YES. IT'S HARD TO TELL ANYMORE.
YOU GOT **THAT** RIGHT..
YOU GOT THAT **WRONG**.
I CAN'T TELL IF YOU'RE SHOWING A WELL-BALANCED OUTLOOK, OR PITIFUL INDECISIVENESS
ME NEITHER.
ME TOO...

YOU HAVE A UNIQUE ATTITUDE, IM4U... I'D LIKE TO GET INSIDE THAT HEAD OF YOURS AND SEE WHAT MAKES YOU TICK...
THAT'D BE NICE. I WISH HE COULD!
ARE YOU **KIDDING**? IT'S CROWDED ENOUGH IN HERE ALREADY...

OH-HI, RATLIFF. I WAS WONDERING WHO BORROWED MY TIME MACHINE.

YEAH- I TOOK A QUICK TRIP TO MY CHILDHOOD.
BETTER REMINISCENCE THROUGH TECHNOLOGY.

YUP. AN OCCASIONAL VISIT TO THE GOOD OLD DAYS ALWAYS SEEMS TO GIVE ME A FRESH PERSPECTIVE ON THE PRESENT.
WHAT ARE YOU DOING NOW?

I SPILLED A PACK OF CRACKER-JACKS ON THE WAY BACK.
YOU CAN'T GO HOME AGAIN IF YOU'RE STILL THERE.

LOOK, BETH- RATLIFF IS ON TV!
MY MAN!
AT BRAND X, WE'RE HUGE, BUT OUR MEGA-ENORMITY DOESN'T KEEP US FROM CARING..
NEW STREAM COMICS
©87 Sam Hurt

YOU REALLY LIKE GOING WITH A FAMOUS GUY, DON'T YOU?
IN HIGHSCHOOL, NOBODY EVER THOUGHT I'D MAKE IT BIG LIKE THIS!
OUR PRODUCTS SHOW OUR PRIDE... FROM OUR HUSBAND-PLEASING BISCUITS TO OUR STATE-OF-THE-ART TELECOMMUNICATION SATELLITES...

THIS IS THE LAND OF OPPORTUNITY, BETH. ANYBODY CAN GROW UP TO BE FIRST LADY...
YOU'RE RIGHT, SALLY. DREAMS HAVE NO LIMITS...
THERE'S NO REST WHEN YOU'RE STRIVING FOR EXCELLENCE, RIGHT, GRANDMA X?
-NOW WITH MORE BUTTERY TASTE...

MY NEW JOB WITH BRAND X HAS TURNED MY LIFE AROUND, BETH...
MY GUY IS FAMOUS! I SAW YOUR COMMERCIAL ON TV, RATLIFF.
NEW STREAM COMICS
©87 Sam Hurt

JUST THINK: ME, WORKING WITH GRANDMA X... THE GRANDMA X!
JUST THINK: ME, GOING OUT WITH YOU... THE YOU!..

LIFE IS FUNNY- YOU STUMBLE ALONG, GETTING BY... THEN SOMETHING LIKE BRAND X COMES ALONG AND CHANGES EVERYTHING...

I DOUBT ANYONE ELSE COULD EXPRESS IT QUITE LIKE YOU...

!!
TIC
BRAND X

SAY- WHAT EVER HAPPENED TO ROD? I HAVEN'T SEEN HIM AROUND IN A WHILE...
YEAH... HE USED TO ALWAYS COME AROUND AND BRAG ABOUT HIS BIG-DEAL JOB WITH TIC- "THREE INITIAL COMPANY"...

THAT'S RIGHT! LAST TIME I SAW HIM, HE WAS FREAKING OUT BECAUSE BRAND X WAS ATTEMPTING A HOSTILE TAKEOVER OF TIC...
I WONDER HOW IT ALL CAME OUT...
©87 Sam Hurt

HELLO, BRAND X... THREE INITIAL DIVISION...

©87 HUK
IT'S NOT WHERE YOU GO- IT'S HOW YOU GET THERE...
HEY! I WAS ABOUT TO SIT IN THAT CHAIR!

LOOK WHAT I FOUND FOR YOU, PEACHES... A **CHAIR** JUST YOUR SIZE!

THINK OF THE CRAFTSMEN WHO MADE THAT CHAIR... THEY MADE IT FOR A GROWNUP-SIZED PERSON. YOU DON'T WANT THEIR EXTRA WORK TO GO TO WASTE, DO YOU?
©87 HUK

OK- I DIDN'T WANT TO HAVE TO DO THIS, BUT **I'M** THE ADULT, **YOU'RE** THE CHILD. TRADE CHAIRS WITH ME. **NOW**!

AT LEAST I HAVE THE SATISFACTION OF KNOWING I TRIED EVERYTHING...

HEY, LADY- WHAT'S THE DEAL WITH THAT CONTRAPTION?
IT'S THE EXTRATERRESTRIAL EQUIVALENT OF ELEVATOR SHOES. IT'S CONSTRUCTED FROM TITANIUM, MINED FROM A DEAD STAR IN THE CRAB NEBULA...

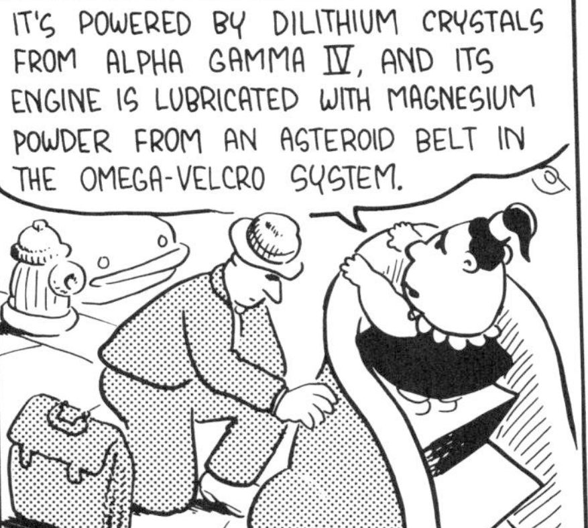
IT'S POWERED BY DILITHIUM CRYSTALS FROM ALPHA GAMMA IV, AND ITS ENGINE IS LUBRICATED WITH MAGNESIUM POWDER FROM AN ASTEROID BELT IN THE OMEGA-VELCRO SYSTEM.
5-20

SOME PEOPLE JUST CAN'T SEEM TO BUY AMERICAN...

EYEBEAM
WELL, SHE HASN'T BEEN AROUND FOR A **REAL** LONG TIME.
TRUE. MAYBE IT'S TIME FOR SOME OFFICIAL POLICY CHANGES.
©07 Sam Hurt
YEAH! LIKE EVERYBODY GETS TO BE BOSS!
OK: I HEREBY MOVE THAT THIS CLUB BE RUN DEMOCRATICALLY EVERYBODY GETS A SAY.

I DOUBLE SECOND THAT MOTION WITH NO TAKE-BACKS! THAT MAKES IT O-
WHF

DID I MISS ANYTHING?
NOTHING, O QUEEN.

YOU SAY I MISSED NOTHING?
WITHOUT YOU, WE WERE LEADERLESS AND UNABLE TO ACT, O QUEEN...

AW, C'MON - YOU COULD'VE FOUND SOMETHING TO DO! LIKE MAYBE, ERECTING A STATUE IN MY HONOR...

HEY... THAT'S NOT A BAD IDEA...

I THINK WE'RE GOING TO NEED MORE MUD.

I'M GOING OUT TO PLAY, UNCLE RATLIFF...
OK- BUT YOU'D BETTER BE BACK BY FIVE.

I'LL COME BACK WHEN I'M THROUGH PLAYING. FAIR ENOUGH?
I'M SERIOUS. IF YOU'RE NOT BACK BY FIVE, I'LL HAVE TO TAKE AWAY THAT TRICYCLE/ CHARIOT OF YOURS...

YOU WOULDN'T BE TRYING TO CROWD ME, WOULD YOU?
WELL, NO, PEACHES... I JUST...

THAT'S GOOD. CHECK YOU LATER.
SO MUCH FOR USING THAT THING AS A DISCIPLINARY TOOL...

WATCH OUT! HERE SHE COMES!

WE OFFER OUR HUMBLE GREETINGS, O QUEEN.
YOU MAY RISE.

OK, LET'S PLAY.
WHAT GAME WOULD PLEASE YOU, O QUEEN?

OH **GREAT!** THAT'S 86-0!
QUIT COMPLAINING! IT'S TWO AGAINST ONE...

EYEBEAM
NOTICE
NUDE BEACH
THAT'S FUNNY- I HEARD THIS WAS **THE** PLACE TO SHOCK AND BE SHOCKED...
©87 SAM HURT

NICE PARTY
YES. THE VIEW FROM THIS TERRACE IS MARVELOUS!
SAY- AREN'T YOU NICOLE BODOLUX? I WATCH YOUR SHOW ON OCCASION.
OH, I **HOPED** YOU WERE WATCHING! I HAD THIS HUGE CRUSH ON YOU IN THIRD GRADE.
WAS THAT YOU? HEY- I HAVE A PLACE WITH A VERY NICE VIEW. I COULD DRIVE US THERE...
GREAT!
WHAT THE HECK- THIS IS OBVIOUSLY A DREAM... I MIGHT GET LUCKY!...
HEY... **NICE** CAR!
©87 Sam Hurt

HI, HO AND-
SPLUT
SPUTTER
FIZZLE

HEY! THIS IS NO GOOD! IT WON'T GO!

WHAT'LL I DO NOW? HOW CAN I EVEN GET IT TO THE SHOP? OH, YEAH!
©88 SAM HURT
1-27

MUSH! MUSH!
SERIOUSLY. IT'S TIME WE STARTED THINKING UNION!
JOE'S
AUTO SERVICE

WE FOUND YOUR PROBLEM, MA'AM, BUT WE CAN'T FIX IT FOR ABOUT A MONTH OR SO.
A MONTH? BUT I HAVE MONEY. I FOUND MY UNCLE RATLIFF'S WALLET.
WIPER BLADES
YOU WANT IT WHEN?

IT'S NOT A MONEY PROBLEM. YOUR SCOOTER, OR WHATEVER YOU CALL IT, IS AN IMPORT. IT'S A PARTS PROBLEM.
A PARTS PROBLEM?
WIPER BLADES
TOM'S SNACKS
©88 SAM HURT
1-28

WE DON'T KEEP DILITHIUM CRYSTALS IN STOCK.
WIPER BLADES
FUSES
Snacks

NEED A JUMP START? I HAVE SOME CABLES.
OH, BLESS YOU! I THOUGHT I WAS GOING TO BE STUCK HERE ALL DAY.

...AND...A LITTLE FURTHER... COME ON... OK. THAT'S GOOD.
©88 Sam Hurt

LATER
ONCE AGAIN, THANKS! THIS WAS SO HELPFUL. I REALLY -HEY, WHAT'S THE MATTER?
3-11

THIS IS MY SIDEWALK. SORRY, BUT NO GIRLS ALLOWED ON MY SIDEWALK...
©98 Sam Hurt 1-20
SORRY, BUT NO SEXIST PIGLETS ALLOWED ON MY PLANET...
uuuuuuuugh...

YOU KNOW, IT'S NOT A SAFE WORLD ANYMORE.
IT'S SAD. EVERY DAY IN THE PAPER YOU READ ABOUT AN ASSAULT WITH A DEADLY WEAPON...
YEAH... IF ONLY- LOOK OUT!
WHAT'S THE MATTER?
YA!
©97 Sam Hurt
YIP ARF
ARF
YIP
RUN, SALLY, RUN
SOMEBODY GET HELP— IT'S A PIT CHIHUAHUA!
YIP ARF

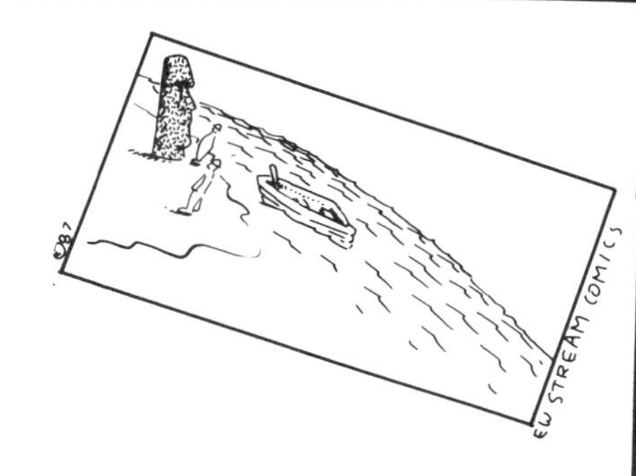

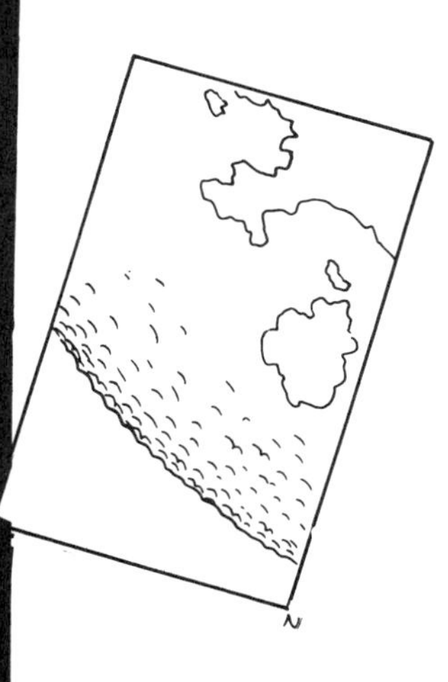

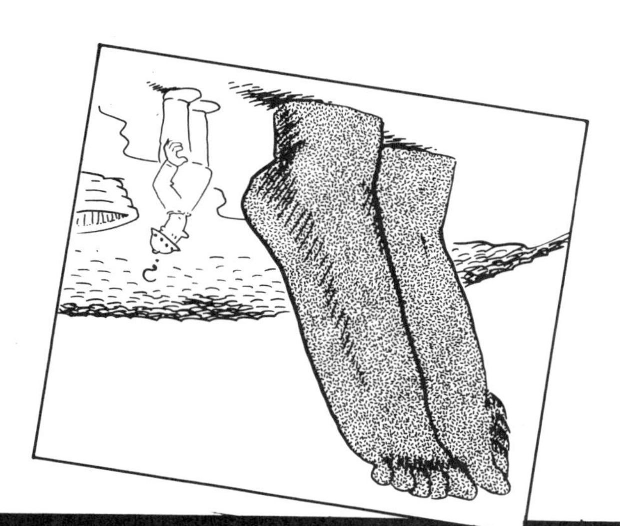

EYEBEAM

IS MY TRICYCLE FIXED YET?
HOLD ON, MA'AM. LET ME CHECK.
FAN BELTS
FUSES
WIPER BLADES
IF IT'S IN STOCK, WE'VE GOT IT!
YOU WANT IT WHEN?

HEY, ZACK-- HOW'S IT GOING WITH THAT IMPORT?
I'M NOT SURE, ED. THESE LUG-NUTS DON'T SEEM TO BE METRIC **OR** NORMAL...
WIPERS
N GOD WE TRUST ALL OTHERS MUST PAY CASH!

REALLY?
YEAH. AND ALL THE BOLTS ON THIS SIDE OF THE THING HAVE A LEFT-HAND THREAD!
AW, **COME ON**!
AL DIDN'T BELIEVE IT, EITHER.
©88 Sam Hurt

I SURE DIDN'T. BUT SEE FOR YOURSELF!
WELL, I'LL BE!
YOU KNOW WHO COULD FIGURE THIS OUT? OLD MAN WITHER- OH, HELLO, MR. WITHERSPOON!
QUIT YAMMERIN AND HOLD THIS LIGHT FOR ME!
YES, SIR!
YES, SIR!
PISTON WEEK

I'M SERIOUS! I SAW HER YESTERDAY. **SHE DIDNT HAVE IT.**
YOU'RE TRYING TO TELL ME HER SCOOTER / CHARIOT IS STILL IN THE SHOP?
Sam Hurt ©88

IF I'M LYING, MAY I BE KISSED BY MISS APPLEBUTT!
HEY! THERE SHE IS! NO CHARIOT! NO TRICYCLE EVEN!

LOOKS LIKE THE TABLES ARE TURNED!
LOOKS LIKE IT'S TIME FOR A LONG OVERDUE EVENING OF THE SCORE.

LOOKS LIKE I'LL BE ABLE TO GET AROUND UNTIL IT GETS OUT OF THE SHOP.

JUST A MINUTE, LADY. LET ME CHECK...
OUR FIRST FANBELT.
IN GOD WE TRUST ALL OTHERS MUST PAY
Sam Hurt ©88

LADY WANTS TO KNOW IF HER "CHARIOT" IS READY...
OH- SHE MEANS THAT LITTLE FOREIGN SCOOTER JOB. WE GOT ALL THE PARTS IN, BUT LARRY HERE IS STILL PUTTING IT TOGETHER. HOW'S IT GOING, LARRY?
SLOW, BOYS. NEVER SEEN AN ION-COOLED ENGINE BEFORE...
WIGNUT TODAY

WELL, WHAT DO I TELL THE LADY?
DON'T BE AN **IDIOT**! IT COULD BE WEEKS, COULD BE MONTHS. JUST TRY TO STALL HER- AND **GET OFF MY BACK**!
THROUGH VEGETABLES

WE'LL HAVE IT FOR YOU WEDNESDAY AT THREE O'CLOCK...
I like this guy.

WHAT A STUPID VEHICLE...
ROADSIDE CAFE

ONLY TWO WHEELS. THAT'S NOT VERY STABLE. I'LL BET IT'S VERY EASY FOR IT TO...

YEP.

OOPS.
HEY! YOU KNOCKED MY BIKE OVER!
CAFE

WELL, IT NEVER WOULD'VE HAPPENED IF YOU'D HAD ENOUGH SENSE TO PUT TRAINING WHEELS ON IT.
TRAINING WHEELS...?
...TRAINING WHEELS!?

TRAINING WHEELS?
SPLUTTER... CHOKE...
TRAINING WHEELS!
THE BEST DEFENSE IS TO BE GOOD AND OFFENSIVE...

IT'S READY, MA'AM. I ENDED UP FIXING IT MYSELF. HOLD ON- I'LL GET IT.
OH, BOY!

THOSE OLD GUYS NEVER WOULD'VE FIGURED IT OUT. THEY THOUGHT THEY WERE WORKING ON AN IMPORTED ITALIAN SCOOTER.
OH. AND YOU KNOW WHAT IT REALLY IS?

WELL, IT'S GOTTA BE SOME KIND OF GOVERNMENT EXPERIMENT... AM I RIGHT?
UH... I REALLY CAN'T SAY...

I KNEW IT! IN THAT CASE, THERE WILL BE NO CHARGE.
AND THEY SAY WOMEN ARE AT A DISADVANTAGE IN DEALING WITH MECHANICS...

TRY HER OUT. SHE OUGHT TO BE RUNNING PRETTY SMOOTHLY NOW.
I HOPE SO. I'VE MISSED BEING ABLE TO RIDE AROUND IN STYLE...

HMM. NOT BAD.
PEPPY LITTLE NUMBER ISN'T SHE?

HEY- THIS TRACTOR-BEAM HAS NEVER WORKED BEFORE!
I FIXED THE CRUISE-CONTROL, TOO. CHECK IT OUT.

On the road again
Look out below, I'm on the road again
My favorite pastime's causing havoc now and then
Lock up your dog, I'm on the road again...

Here comes Peter Cottontail
Hopping down the bunny trail
He'll do no more hopping if he gets in Peaches' way

ACTUALLY, I SHOULD BE MORE SERIOUS ABOUT THIS. THIS MACHINE GIVES ME GREAT POWER...

...AND WITH THIS MUCH POWER COMES AN AWESOME RESPONSIBILITY...
HEY, LADY- THEY QUIT MAKING THOSE GOOFY ITALIAN SCOOTERS!

...THAT'S WHY THE WORLD IS FORTUNATE THAT IT FELL INTO MY HANDS.
I WILL RESPECT OTHER PEOPLE'S VEHICLES... I WILL RESPECT OTHER P

BOY IS IT GREAT TO BE BACK ON TOP OF THINGS...

...BUT I WONDER HOW THE TRICYCLE CLUB IS DOING? I HAD TO COMMANDEER THEIR VEHICLES DURING MY RECENT CRISIS. I SHOULD RETURN THEM SO THAT WE ALL MAY RIDE TOGETHER AGAIN.

THEY'LL BE SO GLAD TO SEE ME. I'LL BET THEY'VE MISSED ME. I'LL BET THEY'RE THINKING ABOUT ME RIGHT NOW.

MAY HER SHOELACES BECOME HOPELESSLY TANGLED.
MAY SHE SPILL LEMONADE IN HER LAP AT A BIG PARTY!

FIRST, A GIRL TAKES OVER THE TRICYCLE CLUB, THEN SHE TAKES AWAY OUR TRIKES...
THE WORST PART OF IT IS HOW WE GROVELLED BEFORE HER LIKE SPINELESS WORMS...

I HARDLY SEE THE POINT OF GOING ON.
LITTLE BOYS WITHOUT WHEELS. IT'S A GRIM PORTRAIT IN DESOLATION AND DESPAIR...

HI, FELLOWS, I'M THROUGH WITH THESE...
BEHOLD!
LO!

BEING A LOYAL SUBJECT PAYS OFF UNDER MY ADMINISTRATION.
YOU HAVE BLESSED US, O QUEEN!

THIS IS SO GREAT! WE'VE GOT OUR TRIKES BACK!
IT'S LIKE A WELCOME-HOME PARTY FOR MY BUTT.

BUT NOW THAT WE HAVE WHEELS, WE MUST RIDE. WE MUST RIDE LONG AND HARD.
YES. WE MUST RIDE TO A PLACE WHERE "SHE" CAN NEVER RULE OVER US AGAIN.

WE MUST LEAVE THIS PLACE FAR, FAR BEHIND.
WE MUST RIDE UNTIL SHE IS A MERE SPECK ON THE HORIZON OF OUR PAST.

OH, HI! WHAT ARE YOU FELLOWS DOING WAY OUT HERE?
AH! THERE YOU ARE!

COME ON! THE THREE TRICYCLATEERS CAN NOW RIDE AGAIN!
oh boy
great
©88 Sam Hurt

LET US ROLL TOGETHER DOWN THE SIDEWALK OF LIFE! FREER THAN THE WINDS, WE GLIDE ALONG AS SMOOTHLY AS CLOUDS SLIPPING THROUGH THE MIDNIGHT SKY...
Yeah
Right

HALT, MEN. I SPY AN OASIS OF SORTS - A WAY STATION, HOUSING A TREASURE TROVE OF NOURISHMENT AND SATISFACTION!
SOUNDS GOOD. MAYBE WE SHOULD STOP THERE.
4-6

BRILLIANT STRATEGY.
ELEVEN
7-Ele
HOME OF THE MEGA-GULP

THE MIND REELS...
SO MUCH CANDY. SO LITTLE TIME.
M+Ms
DOTS
JU-JU
GUMBO
NEW! SMUDGIE
GLOOPERS
©88 Sam Hurt

TO CHOOSE ONE IS TO GIVE UP ALL THE OTHERS. IT'S ENOUGH TO DRIVE ONE MAD!
A SANE MAN HAS ONLY ONE CHOICE: SYSTEMATIC GLUTTONY.
BERNIES
4-7

AN INTERESTING SOLUTION; BUT ONE THAT WOULD WORK BETTER IF TRICYCLES HAD TRUNKS.
TRUE.
DON'T WORRY, MEN- THERE'S STILL PLENTY OF ROOM IN MY CARGO BAY...

BRAND X
WELCOME TO BRAND X VILLAGES DISTINCTIVE HOUSING
- BRAND X -
XMOBILE
BRAND X PUTTY
BRAND X
BRAND X GRAVEL
BRAND X SNAIL CHOW
BRAND X ORGANIC PEANUT BUTTER
BRAND X RADIOACTIVE GLUE
BRAND X INDUSTRIAL STREGNTH SLUDGE

"LIFESTYLES OF THE POOR AND OBSCURE" WILL RETURN AFTER THIS...

OUT HERE ON THE RANCH, OUR FAVORITE CHOW IS GRANDMA X'S DOWN-HOME TOASTER-STEAKS, NOW CREAM GRAVY-FILLED! YOUR TUMMY WILL BE TICKLED PINK!

MAYBE FUTURE GENERATIONS WILL APPRECIATE MY WORK...

I GUESS WE'VE **ALL** NOTICED THAT "BRAND X" PRODUCTS ARE... WELL, A LITTLE SPECIAL...
BRAND X PARTICLES
BRAND X
BRAND X
CHUNKS
BRAND X
PEACH FUZZ
BRAND X
BRAND X
BREAKFAST SWIRLS
BRAND X

THERE'S A REASON... A REASON FOR THAT **X**TRA ATTENTION TO DETAIL; A **REASON** FOR THAT WARM, HUMAN TOUCH THAT DISTINGUISHES ALL BRAND X PRODUCTS:
BRAND X

.. **GRANDMA** X!
BISCUIT?

EYEBEAM
IT ALL BEGAN IN A LITTLE CABIN BACK IN 1893...

GRANDMA X WAS YOUNGER THEN, BUT SHE ALREADY KNEW THE FORMULA FOR SUCCESS: SHE BAKED A LITTLE **LOVE** INTO EVERYTHING SHE MADE...
Sam Hurt ©87

AT **BRAND X**, WE KNOW BETTER THAN TO CHANGE A WINNING FORMULA...
BRAND X
BRAND X DOG FOOD
BRAND X TAR PAPER
BRAND X CORN FLAKES

...SO WE'VE **CONTINUED** IN THAT TRADITION OF HAND-MADE QUALITY AND EXTRA CARE, SO **YOU** DON'T HAVE TO BOTHER!
-RIGHT, GRANDMA X?
RIGHT, SONNY!
BRAND X MUFFIN IN A CAN

GRANDMA X STARTED OUT IN A LITTLE CABIN IN THE WOODS...
BUT WORD GOT AROUND, AND DEMAND GREW. GRANDMA X NOW HAS A DEDICATED STAFF HELPING HER.
AND OF COURSE, SHE'S ADDED ON TO THE KITCHEN.
OH LORDY. IT'S TUESDAY. I HAVE TO MOP.
BRAND X
©87 SAM HURT

IT WENT WELL TODAY, SONNY. IT'LL BE A COMMERCIAL WE CAN BE PROUD OF.
I'M PROUD JUST TO BE WORKING WITH YOU, MA'AM! JUST THINK: **THE** GRANDMA X!
IT'S A THRILL, ALRIGHT. I NEARLY **FAINTED** WHEN THEY TOLD ME I GOT THE PART...
THAT'S GREAT. HEY, I'LL SEE YOU TOMORROW, GRANDMA X.
...."GOT THE PART"?!
NEW STREAM COMICS
©87 SAM HURT

EYEBEAM
HI, EYEBEAM. I RECOVERED FROM MY SHATTERED ILLUSION.
GOOD. YOU WERE REELING WITH DISENCHANTMENT WHEN YOU FOUND OUT GRANDMA X WAS JUST AN ACTRESS.
NOW, I REALIZE THAT MILDRED REPRESENTS THE SPIRIT OF GRANDMA X: KINDNESS, CONCERN FOR QUALITY, ... ETC.
GOOD! SO EVERYTHING'S OK NOW...
©87 Sam Hurt New Stream Comics
YEAH... EXCEPT I FEEL A LITTLE SILLY FOR HAVING BEEN SO NAIVE...
DON'T WORRY- WE ALL GO THROUGH THAT. I MYSELF WAS ALMOST 15 BEFORE I FOUND OUT THAT PRO WRESTLING IS ALL A BIG ACT.
HUH...? WHA...?
...OOPS...

EYEBEAM
WHO...? WHA...? HUH...?
WHAT'S THE MATTER WITH RATLIFF?
LOOKS LIKE HE'S SUFFERING FROM A SHATTERED ILLUSION...
NEW STREAM COMICS
©87 HURT
WHAT COULD'VE CAUSED THAT?
I DON'T KNOW MAYBE HE FOUND OUT THAT HIS IDOL, GRANDMA X, IS JUST AN ACTRESS...
WHUH..? WHE..? WHY...?
OH, THE PAIN! OH, THE STINGING DISAPPOINTMENT! OH, THE BITTER PSYCHIC BRUISING OF A SHATTERED ILLUSION!
ON THE OTHER HAND, IT COULD JUST BE A BAD SPRAIN...
HUH...WHA... HMMM...

SO, ANYWAY, I MAKE COMMERCIALS. I EXPLAIN HOW GRANDMA X HAS BEEN BAKING HER FAMOUS "MUFFIN IN A CAN" FOR THREE GENERATIONS...

OF COURSE, "GRANDMA X" IS REALLY JUST AN ACTRESS FROM FLORIDA. HER NAME IS MILDRED FRAP.

DON'T TELL ME. IN REAL LIFE, SHE'S NOT MUCH OF A COOK.
THE WOMAN WOULDN'T KNOW SHORTENING FROM SHINOLA...

BENDING WIRE WITH PRIDE FOR THREE GENERATIONS, RIGHT, GRANDMA X?
GOOD, OLD-FASHIONED QUALITY. THERE'S JUST NO SUBSTITUTE!

SO REMEMBER- WHEN YOU THINK CHAIN LINK, THINK BRAND X!
YOU HAVE TO ADMIT, IT **DOES** HAVE A CERTAIN RING TO IT...
DING DONG

NOW, WHO COULD THAT BE? SOME SALEMAN? A STRAY PIZZA IN SEARCH OF A HOME? A CO-WORKER?

HEY- IT'S **YOU**!
DROPPING IN ON PEOPLE UNEXPECTEDLY FOR THREE GENERATIONS.

OH, LORDY. I'M SO TIRED. I'VE BEEN BAKING THOSE DELICIOUS MUFFINS OF MINE ALL DAY...

THEN, ON TO THE PACKAGING DEPARTMENT. WE SEAL THEM UP TIGHT SO THEY'LL STAY DOWN-HOME FRESH!
HEY, GRANDMA X- -I MEAN MILDRED- WE'RE NOT MAKING A COMMERCIAL NOW. YOU CAN RELAX AND BE YOURSELF...

OH... WELL, MY-MY...

GOT ANY BEER THEN?
WHAT KIND OF HOST **AM** I?

YOU KNOW, GRANDMA X, IN THE COMMERCIALS, THEY SAY YOU STARTED OUT IN A LITTLE COTTAGE IN THE WOODS...
I KNOW YOU'RE REALLY AN ACTRESS, BUT THAT IMAGE JUST FITS YOU SOMEHOW... ANYTHING TO IT?
WELL... SORT OF...
...I REALLY STARTED OUT IN AN AIRSTREAM CAMPER NEAR A TRAILER PARK ON THE EDGE OF TOWN.
CLOSE ENOUGH.
LIFE IS TOO SHORT TO HAGGLE OVER TRIVIAL DETAILS...

YOU SURE LIVE CLOSE TO WORK, RATLIFF.
IT'S PRETTY HANDY, GRANDMA X. - JUST A TEN MINUTE DRIVE.
I NOTICED YOU HAVE AN EXTRA ROOM. HOW'D YOU LIKE TO RENT IT OUT?
WELL, I COULD USE THE MONEY... BUT I'M NOT SURE YOU'D FIT IN.
I DON'T PLAY SHUFFLEBOARD, IF THAT'S WHAT YOU'RE WORRIED ABOUT.
I JUST WANT TO MAKE SURE YOU KNOW WHAT YOU'RE GETTING INTO.
GIT ALONG THERE. **HYA**!
MOO.
LIKE MY HAIR? I GOT A **PERM WAVE**.
YEAH. I FOLLOWED YOU HOME. I PASSED A LOT OF SEASICK BYSTANDERS.

DO YOU REALLY WANT TO LIVE HERE, GRANDMA X?
OH, YES. I'M MAKING ENOUGH MONEY NOW TO MOVE UP IN THE WORLD.
MOVE UP? TO **THIS** PLACE? THIS IS A MOVE UP? YOU MUST BE LIVING IN A REAL DUMP!
YOU MIGHT SAY THAT...
EXIT HERE
HARVEST TIME RETIREMENT COMMUNITY
VACANCY

WELL, GRANDMA X, IF YOU'RE GOING TO LIVE HERE, I'D BETTER INTRODUCE YOU AROUND.
SURE. LET'S GET CRACKING.

THE QUEEN OF THE UNIVERSE HAS LEARNED OF AN ATTEMPT BY ONE OF HER CLOSEST FOLLOWERS TO OVERTHROW HER GOVERNMENT...

TO FIND OUT WHICH ONE IT IS, SHE WILL USE HER POWERFUL MIND-BEAM TO CREATE AN ILLUSION OF HORRIBLE GIANTS. THIS WILL FRIGHTEN A CONFESSION OUT OF HER BETRAYER...

AND THIS IS LITTLE PEACHES, MY NIECE. SAY HELLO, PEACHES.
LOOKS LIKE WE **STARTLED** THE POOR DEAR...
WHA!

AND THIS IS MY LITTLE NEPHEW, TYKIE
OH. I DIDN'T KNOW YOU HAD A BABY LIVING HERE.

YES. ACTUALLY, THIS IS A PRETTY WELL-ROUNDED HOUSEHOLD.
OH, ISN'T HE A WITTLE SUGAR-PLUM? 'ES, HE IS!

IS HE GWAMMY'S WITTLE PWESHIOUS? 'ES, 'E IS! IS HIM UM TUMMY WITTO SNOOKUMS? UBBY WUBBY UBBY WUBBY! GOOBY GOOGY **GOOKIE**!

EXCUSE ME, GRANDMA X, BUT WE'VE DECIDED TO TEACH THIS ONE ENGLISH...
OH. SORRY.
TA!

I'D LIKE TO CHECK OUT PLEASE...
WHAT?
HARVEST TIME RETIREMENT COMMUNITY

I'M MOVING I'M NOT GOING TO LIVE HERE ANYMORE.
BUT, MA'AM- THIS IS YOUR **HOME**! WE HAVE ONE OF THE BEST FACILITIES IN THE COUNTRY. YOU **CAN'T** JUST LEAVE!

JUST WATCH ME! THIS PLACE SMELLS LIKE A HOSPITAL. I'M OUT OF HERE.
MR. JONES, LET'S KEEP THE NICE LADY ON THE GROUNDS UNTIL HER LITTLE CONFUSION SPELL PASSES...

I CAN USE MY KNEES AND ELBOWS TO GIVE YOU A CONFUSION SPELL YOU WON'T FORGET.
UH...LET ME HELP YOU WITH THAT DOOR.
OH, AND BY THE WAY, WE DON'T ALLOW PETS!

EYEBEAM
OK, GRANDMA X- GET READY. THE NEXT PERSON YOU'RE GOING TO MEET IS.......A LITTLE DIFFERENT. HE'S.... WELL, HE'S A ROBOT.
AH... SOUNDS NEW FANGLED..
I JUST THOUGHT I OUGHT TO TRY TO PREPARE YOU BEFOREHAND...
OH, COME NOW, RATLIFF- I'M A GROWN WOMAN! I'VE BEEN AROUND. IT'S HARD TO GET ME FLUSTERED!
OK, THEN- GRANDMA X, MEET IM4U.
AH... JE SUIS ENCHANTÉ, MA CHÉRIE...
OH! MY GOODNESS! MY, OH MY! HEAVENS TO BETSY! OH, LORDY... GOODNESS ME! WELL WELL WELL...!
©87 Sambo

EYEBEAM
HEY, OSGOOD- WHAT'S IT LIKE, BEING A CAT? I MEAN YOU'RE A MEMBER OF THE SPECIES THAT PEOPLE ALWAYS INSIST ON TREATING AS HUMAN...
YOU'RE RIGHT. STUPID QUESTION...
©87 Sambo Hurt

I BRING MY SPACESHIP TO A HALT. THE CRUMPLED, LIFELESS BODY OF THE EMISSARY FROM ONARA FLOATS IN THE ICY STILLNESS OF SPACE. ANOTHER INNOCENT VICTIM OF THE TOYOTAN CONFLICT.

AFTER REVIVING THE ONARAN EMISSARY, WE CONTINUE TOWARDS THE INTERPLANETARY CONFERENCE ON TOYOTAN VIOLENCE. -WAIT- WHAT'S THAT? UH-OH!
©87 Sam Hurt

IT'S A TOYOTAN WARRIOR! THIS IS IT! TIME TO SHOW THESE SPACE-BULLIES THAT WE STAND UNITED AGAINST THEIR OPPRESSIVE MILITARY REGIME!
5-20

SOMETIMES I THINK THESE ONARAN EMISSARIES ARE A LITTLE TOO PEACE-LOVING...
THUMP
THUMP
THUMP

NO LITTERING
NO LOITERING
IF YOU LIVED HERE, YOU'D BE HOME NOW!
IF YOU CAN READ THIS, YOU'RE TOO CLOSE
BEWARE OF SHAR
BEWARE OF DOG
5-16

GRANDMA X-WHO AM I? WHAT AM I?
WHAT ARE YOU GETTING AT, RATLIFF?
©87 Sam Hurt

I MEAN, AM I SOME AMORPHOUS COLLECTION OF MATTER AND BRAIN-WAVE PATTERNS? A LOOSE BUNDLE OF ATTRIBUTES THAT CHANGES A LITTLE EVERY DAY...?

...OR AM I DEFINED BY THE CONTRAST I MAKE WITH MY SURROUNDINGS? AM I SIMPLY THE PLACE WHERE THE REST OF THE UNIVERSE LEAVES OFF?

SORRY. I GUESS I WAS GETTING EXISTENTIAL AGAIN...
OH, GOOD! I THOUGHT MY EYES WERE GOING!

PEACHES, DEARIE- TIME FOR YOUR NAP...
I'M AFRAID THAT'S UTTERLY OUT OF THE QUESTION.

"UTTERLY"- WHAT AN UNCOMPROMISING WORD. IT LEAVES NO POSSIBILITY THAT YOU'LL RECONSIDER...
ALL **RIGHT**! PUT ME DOWN AND I'LL RECONSIDER A NAP...

FAIR ENOUGH. I THINK THAT ONCE YOU- **HEY!**
WHOOC

DING
ROUND 1

OK- YOU FOOLED ME YESTERDAY, PEACHES, BUT TODAY, YOU **ARE** GOING TO TAKE THAT NAP.
HARDLY SEEMS LIKELY...

NOT- LIKELY? WE'LL SEE.
ZIP
SO SHE TASTED THE SECOND BOWL OF PORRIDGE. "OH, DEAR," SHE EXCLAIMED, "THIS IS COLD AS ICE!"
WHOEVER HEARD OF PUTTING SHOCK ABSORBERS IN A CAT DOOR..?

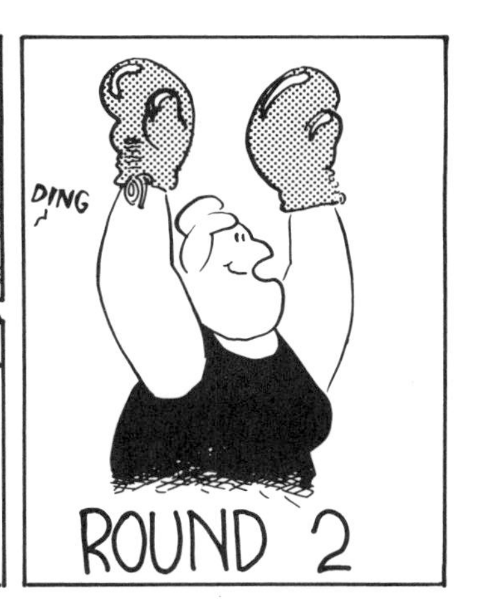
DING
ROUND 2

COME NOW, PEACHES- TIME FOR YOUR NAP.
YOU KNOW, GRANDMA X, THAT NAP YESTERDAY WAS A PLEASANT SURPRISE. I ACTUALLY **ENJOYED** IT!

SO C'MON, LET'S- HA! FOOLED YOU!
MAYBE NOT- TODAY I CAME PREPARED...
WHOOOOSHHH

YOU'LL **NEVER** CATCH ME!
YOU'LL NEVER **ESCAPE**
ONE SIDE, EVERYBODY. WIDE LOAD!

DING
ROUND 3

EYEBEAM

EYEBEAM

RRRRRRR
STOP THAT! I **WON'T** HAVE YOU ATTACKING MY HOUSEGUESTS, PEACHES!

RRRRRRRRRRRRRRRR
YOU CAN'T DO JUST ANYTHING YOU WANT, YOU KNOW...
©88 Sam Hurt

OH, YEAH? WELL, IN CASE YOU HAVEN'T HEARD, THIS IS **SUPPOSED** TO BE A FREE COUNTRY.
I'M GOING TO HAVE TO THINK OF A WAY TO TEACH HER THAT IT'S NOT THAT SIMPLE...

LATER...
MY ♪ COUNTRY 'TIS OF THEE ♪

...SWEET LAND OF LIBERTY
A PROCLAMATION OF PATRIOTISM?

OH, LAND SAKES!
PERHAPS, AN ENDEAVOR TO RESOLVE DIFFERENCES. A SMALL STEP TOWARDS MUTUAL UNDERSTANDING.

ULTIMATELY, AN AGREEMENT TO DISAGREE.

EYEBEAM

WERE YOU AND PEACHES HAVING A FUSS? I THOUGHT I HEARD SOME COMMOTION EARLIER.
OH, IT WAS NOTHING. I THINK SHE WAS A LITTLE FUSSY BECAUSE IT WAS HER NAP TIME.
YOU MEAN YOU TRIED TO TELL HER WHEN TO GO TO SLEEP? WOW!..
OH, IT JUST TAKES A LITTLE ASSERTIVE-NESS... OH, WATCH OUT FOR THE PLACE WHERE WE-
SERIOUSLY, I WISH I COULD'VE SEEN THAT!
OH, DEAR.
NO- I'D RATHER JUST HEAR ABOUT IT...

WHY IS PEACHES SO OUT OF CONTROL, GRANDMA X? IS IT MY FAULT?
YOU MUSTN'T BLAME YOURSELF, RATLIFF. A GUILTY CONSCIENCE CAN DESTROY YOUR ABILITY TO ADMINISTER DISCIPLINE!

I GUESS MAYBE YOU'RE RIGHT...
...AND ANOTHER THING, SHE **NEEDS** THAT DISCIPLINE. WITHOUT IT, SHE WON'T BE ABLE TO COPE WITH ADULT LIFE.
New Stream Comics

SHE'S RIGHT. I'M DOING PEACHES A BIG FAVOR BY LAYING DOWN THE LAW. I NEED TO BE FIRM!

NOW PEACHES, THIS IS FOR YOUR OWN GOOD..
A BAFFLING MIXTURE OF CLICKS, POPS, AND GLOTTAL STOPS, THE ISLANDERS' NATIVE TONGUE SOUNDS MORE LIKE A WIND CHIME FASHIONED OF WICKER AND PIANO WIRE THAN ANY HUMAN LANGUAGE...

LOOK. THERE THEY GO.
YES. THE COOING KOALA BEARS OF LOVE.

WHAT DO YOU THINK OF THAT ROMANCE? I MEAN, RATLIFF AND BETH AS A COUPLE?
STRANGE, ISNT IT? NOBODY WOULD EVER HAVE PREDICTED IT. IN THEIR OWN SICK WAY, ROD AND BETH SEEMED PERFECT FOR EACH OTHER.
THAT'S TRUE, BUT HEY, WHO ARE **WE** TO SECOND GUESS OTHER PEOPLE'S HORMONES?

RIGHT. I GUESS IT TAKES A CERTAIN AMOUNT OF WISDOM TO ACCEPT LOVE WHEREVER YOU CAN FIND IT..
HERE HERE!
NOW NOW!

BETH! MY EFFERVESCENT BUTTERCUP!
RATLIFF! MY DASHING HORMONAL SWIZZLE STICK!
YOU'VE BEEN AWAY FOR A LONG TIME... I'VE **REALLY** MISSED YOU...
I KNOW... I KNOW... ARE WE BY CHANCE ALONE?
©87 Sam Hurt

I DON'T KNOW. LET ME CHECK.

WELL, LOOKS LIKE EVERYBODY'S JUST KIND OF HANGING AROUND THE HOUSE TODAY...
HI RATLIFF.
SIGH...
BANG.

WHAT'S PLANNED FOR LATER? PEACHES, I'LL BET YOU'RE GOING TO PLAY OUTSIDE ALL AFTERNOON...
NOPE. I'M STAYING RIGHT HERE.
©87 Sam Hurt

BUT, WHY? IT'S A BEAUTIFUL DAY OUT!
BECAUSE THERE MUST BE SOMETHING GOOD GOING ON OR YOU WOULDN'T BE TRYING TO GET ME OUT.

BE PATIENT, MY SWEET. THIS COULD TAKE SOME TIME...
GAT'S OKAY. GUT KLEASE HURRY...

WELL, PEACHES WENT OUT HUNTING FOR DEAD SQUIRRELS. WHAT ARE YOUR PLANS, GRANDMA X?
OH, I THINK I'LL JUST STICK AROUND THE HOUSE AND GET SOME PEACE AND QUIET. WHAT ABOUT YOU?
©87 Sam Hurt

OH, ABOUT THE SAME. YOU'RE NOT GOING OUT TO A MOVIE OR SHOPPING OR ANYTHING?
NO. AS I SAID, I'M JUST GOING TO STAY AROUND HERE.

OH, DARN.

LOOKS LIKE HE'S JUST GOING TO BE HANGING OUT ALL DAY...
WHAT TORTURE!

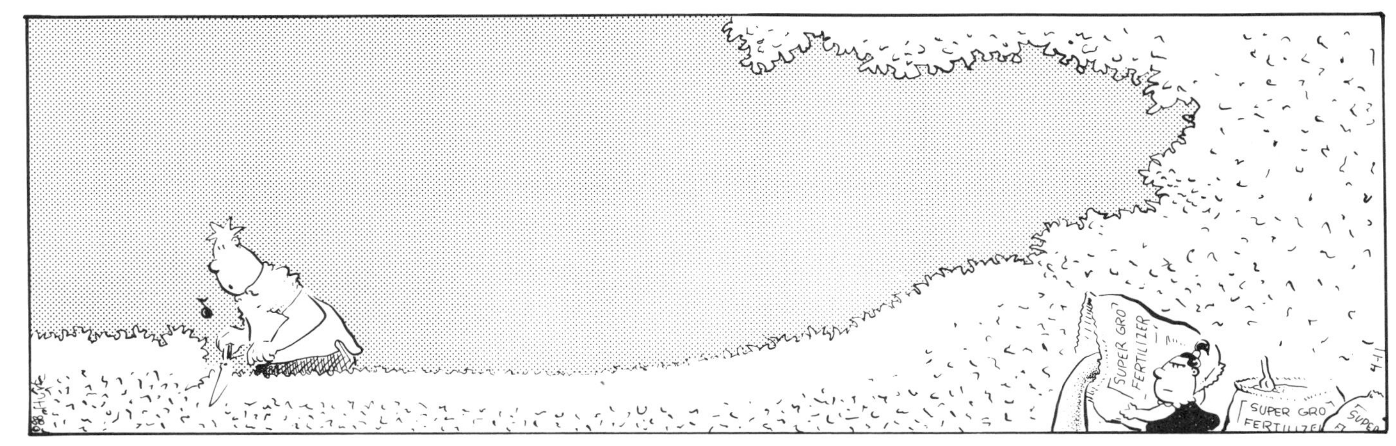
SUPER GRO FERTILIZER
SUPER GRO FERTILIZER

HI THERE, RATLIFF.
BETH! MY FRAGRANT JASMINE BLOSSOM! I MISSED YOU!
SORRY I'VE BEEN GONE SO LONG. I WENT TO A BODY-TONING CAMP.
REALLY? WELL, THAT'S GREAT. -I MEAN, IT'S GREAT TO BE HEALTHY AND ALL.

THANKS. YOU HAVE A GREAT BODY, TOO...
WHAT- THIS OLD THING? SHUCKS...

AS A MATTER OF FACT, WHY DON'T WE DIM THE LIGHTS, PUT ON SOME ELEGANT MUSIC, AND-
YEAH! IT'S BEEN A LONG TIME SINCE-
MUFFIN TIME! LET'S EAT 'EM WHILE THEY'RE HOT!

DAVIS
PLACE 4
RE ELECT JONES
LET'S KEEP
SPUD FOR MAYOR
McGRAW
LEON

RATLIFF- WHAT'S THAT LITTLE OLD LADY DOING HERE? WHY DOES SHE HANG AROUND SO MUCH?
WELL, AFTER ALL, GRANDMA X IS MY HOUSEMATE. SHE LIVES HERE, BETH.

AND WHAT ABOUT THAT ROBOT? HE'S ALWAYS HOGGING UP YOUR E.Z. DUDE RECLINER.
HEY, THIS IS THE MODERN AGE. YOU CAN'T FIGHT PROGRESS.

I DON'T KNOW. I JUST FEEL VAGUELY UNEASY... LIKE MY LIFE ISN'T GOING ANYWHERE.
LOOK- WE ALL FEEL THAT WAY FROM TIME TO TIME...

MAYBE IF YOU HAD A MORE TRADITIONAL BACHELOR PAD...
NOW, LET'S TRY TO FOCUS ON FINDING THE REAL PROBLEM HERE...
JUST UPWIND, TWO GAZELLE PLAY OUT A QUAINT COURTING RITUAL. THEY DRAW CLOSER...CLOSER...

RATLIFF, DID ANYONE EVER TELL YOU YOU HAVE BEAUTIFUL EYES?
POING
WHAT? AWWW...
©88 Sam Hurt

AIGGGHHH! WHAT IS IT? WHAT **IS** IT?
CALM DOWN, BETH. IT'S JUST A TOY ARROW..

GERONIMO.
SORRY. I DIDN'T MEAN TO OVERREACT.
THAT'S OK. WITH KIDS AROUND, YOU GET USED TO THAT SORT OF THING.
3-9

NOW, WHERE WERE WE?
RRRRRRR
RRK!

BETH, I'M SORRY MY NIECE, PEACHES ATTACKED YOU LIKE THAT...
WELL, IT **WAS** A BIT ALARMING.
©88 Sam Hurt

SHE'S A LITTLE WILD, ALRIGHT, BUT WE HAD A GOOD LONG TALK, AND I THINK SHE'LL BEHAVE NOW...
OH, DON'T WORRY ABOUT IT. I... -**HEY!**
BONK

OK, PEACHES. IF THAT'S THE WAY YOU'RE GOING TO BE...
I'M OK- WHAT **WAS** THAT, ANYWAY?
3-14

IT'S ONE OF THOSE DARN WAR TOYS. SOMEHOW, THEY SEEMED MORE INNOCENT WHEN I WAS A KID...
G.I. JOSEPHINE?

PEACHES, YOU DIDN'T BEHAVE VERY WELL AROUND YOUR AUNT BETH. FIRST, YOU PELTED HER WITH SPIT WADS...
©88 Sam Hurt

...THEN YOU FIRED AT HER WITH YOUR PLASTIC BAZOOKA, AND SHOT HER WITH THOSE SUCTION-CUP ARROWS. WHEN SHE FINALLY LEFT, IN TEARS, SHE FOUND HER CAR COVERED WITH WET BATHROOM TISSUE...

I WAS VERY DISAPPOINTED.
MAYBE I WOULDN'T **HAVE** BEHAVIORAL PROBLEMS IF YOU SPENT A LITTLE MORE TIME WITH ME.
3-15

3-15-88
Begin experimentation with a new force, having potential power far greater than any conventional weaponry.

IT SURE HAS WORKED OUT WELL HAVING YOU RENT THE EXTRA ROOM, GRANDMA X...
OH, IT'S JUST BEEN GREAT, RATLIFF. MY WHOLE LIFE HAS CHANGED.

REALLY? THE MOVE'S BEEN GOOD FOR YOU?
OH, MY HEAVENS, YES! YOUR LITTLE NIECE, PEACHES, KEEPS ME FEELING ALIVE. I'VE EVEN STARTED GOING AROUND WITH A YOUNG MAN...

DING DONG
A YOUNG MAN?
EXCUSE ME- THAT'S PROBABLY HIM NOW...

ORGANISMS FOR THE ORGANISM.
ROSES!
I WONDER IF THIS HAS ANYTHING TO DO WITH MY RECENT ELECTRITY BILLS...

MMMM... YES, I SEE. WELL, I JUST THOUGHT I'D CHECK. THANK YOU KINDLY.

WELL, THAT'S DISAPPOINTING.
WHAT'S THE PROBLEM, MILDRED?

THEY TELL ME YOU CAN'T GET ONE OF THOSE ARTIFICIAL HEARTS UNLESS YOU HAVE SOME SORT OF HEALTH PROBLEM.
BUT, WHY ON EARTH WOULD YOU WANT ONE?

I TRY TO BE AS INORGANIC AS POSSIBLE... MY MAN LIKES ME THAT WAY...
I SMELL A PREFABRICATED, PHILANDERING RAT.
HEY- DON'T GO CHANGING ON ME, BABE!

FAREWELL, MY LITTLE BUTTERCUP- PARTING IS SUCH SWEET SORROW- TAKE CARE, AND IF MY GEARS HOLD UP WE'LL MEET AGAIN TOMORROW...

OH, GOODNESS! MY HEART'S ALL A-FLUTTER.
LISTEN, MILDRED, I HATE TO INTERFERE, BUT I'D WATCH OUT FOR THAT GUY. HE'S FICKLE.

THANKS FOR THE TIP, SALLY, BUT I'VE FOUND THAT WITH MEN, YOU HAVE TO SEEK OUT THE GOOD- AND TAKE CARE OF THEM LIKE THEY WERE LITTLE BABIES...
I'M SURE THAT'S GOOD ADVICE. I SHOULDN'T HAVE BUTTED-

OH YEAH- AND DON'T TRUST 'EM ANY FURTHER THAN THE RANGE OF YOUR LARGEST ELECTROMAGNET.
NOW WE'RE TALKIN!

EYEBEAM
ONE LOOK AT YOU AND THE TRANSMISSION FLUID SURGES THROUGH MY BODY. I BECOME GIDDY. MY DRIVE SHAFT SHUDDERS WITH DESIRE...
YOU CHARGE UP MY BATTERIES- YOU SET MY PISTONS ON FIRE... GRANDMA X, YOU'RE THE SPARK IN MY LIFE
YOU CAN CALL ME MILDRED...
......."MILDRED"? NO OFFENSE, BUT IT SOUNDS A LITTLE.... ORGANIC.
"GRANDMA X" IS FINE, TOO...

GRANDMA X, BEING WITH YOU HAS CHANGED MY WHOLE LIFE! THIS... THING WE HAVE GOING- IT'S LIKE A KALEIDOSCOPE- IT HAS SO MANY DIFFERENT FACETS- SO MANY LEVELS...
I MEAN, EVERY FEW MINUTES, I DISCOVER SOME INCREDIBLE NEW ASPECT OF OUR RELATIONSHIP...
LIKE, WHAT?
LIKE, IT COULD GET US ON THE DONAHUE SHOW LIKE THAT!
SNAP
PWNG

EYEBEAM

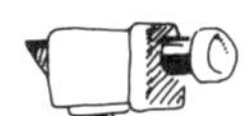

ALLRIGHT, BE PATIENT, PEOPLE- WE'VE GOT A LOT OF WISDOM OUT HERE...

OK: "WHAT'S HAPPENED TO THE OLD-FASHIONED VALUES THAT MADE THIS COUNTRY GREAT? THERE OUGHT TO BE A LAW AGAINST BEING SO ABNORMAL!"
CLAP
CLAP
CLAP
CLAPPITY
CLAP CLAP

"HEY, IT'S NOT FOR ME, BUT IF IT FLOATS THEIR BOAT, MORE POWER TO 'EM. LIVE AND LET LIVE!"
I LOVE TESTING THE WATERS.
CLAP CLAP
OCEAN OF HOUSEWIVES

ROBOTS WITH HUMAN LOVERS. TODAY WE HAVE FIVE COUPLES WHO ARE MAKING A GO AT IT, AND SAY THEIR LIVES ARE RICHER FOR IT.

BUT WE ALSO HAVE A GUEST WHO HAD THE **HORRIFYING** EXPERIENCE OF WATCHING HER ROBOT LOVER MALFUNCTION. AFTER BRINGING HER HOME LATE, IT RAN BOTH OF HER PARENTS THROUGH A FOOD PROCESSOR...

HOW DID THAT MAKE YOU FEEL? I MEAN, I GUESS IT WAS JUST SO AWFUL THAT WORDS ARE NO USE. I MEAN, IT MUST BE IMPOSSIBLE TO EXPRESS THE ABSOLUTE HORROR THAT YOU MUST FEEL EVERY MOMENT OF YOUR LIFE. I MEAN, I'LL BET A DAY NEVER GOES BY WHEN YOU DON'T RELIVE IT.
THAT'S RIGHT.

AND THERE YOU HAVE IT. WE'LL BE RIGHT BACK.

WHAT GOES ON BEHIND THE HEADLINES? BEHIND THE RUMORS? BEHIND OTHER PEOPLE'S CLOSED DOORS? INQUIRING MINDS WANT TO KN- I MEAN, "GERALDO" IS THE SHOW THAT PUTS YOU THERE. C'MON- LET'S GO IN...

OK- FOLLOW CLOSE, BOYS GET READY TO TIGHTEN IN FOR A CLOSE-UP

HERE WE ARE. THIS IS REAL. THIS IS NOW. THIS IS THE RAW, GRAPHIC TRUTH. ...AND I'M GERALDO.
ARE YOU SURE YOU WOULDN'T LIKE SOME TEA?
NO, THANKS.

Ratliff's
Pet Peeves Illustrated

RAPUNZEL, RAPUNZEL, LET DOWN YOUR HAIR!
SORRY, BUD, YOU MUST HAVE THE WRONG APARTMENT.

YOU KNOW, RATLIFF, I KNOW YOU AND BETH ARE A BIG ITEM, BUT I DON'T SEE YOU TOGETHER MUCH.
THAT'S TRUE, BUT YOU SEE, OUR RELATIONSHIP HAS MATURED TO A POINT WHERE WE DON'T HAVE TO SPEND ALL OF OUR TIME TOGETHER

I SEE.
...JUST KNOWING THAT WE'RE SO PERFECT FOR EACH OTHER; THAT SHE'S OUT THERE THINKING OF ME AT THIS VERY MOMENT - IT GIVES ME A SENSE OF SECURITY LIKE I'VE NEVER EXPERIENCED BEFORE!

MEANWHILE...
OH. EXCUSE ME.
EXCUSE **ME**.
CLUNK

I'M SO SORRY I BUMPED INTO YOUR CART.
YOU MUSTN'T APOLOGIZE. YOU'VE MADE MY DAY. BY THE WAY, HAVEN'T WE MET?

I BELIEVE WE MET THROUGH MY FORMER BOYFRIEND, ROD. I'M BETH HOUSTON.
LANCE TROUSERS, esq AT YOUR SERVICE.

NICE SEEING YOU AGAIN. I'D BETTER GET BACK TO MY SHOPPING NOW.
YOU **DID** SAY "FORMER"...

YES. "FORMER". I'VE HEARD A LOT ABOUT YOU LANCE.
WON'T YOU ALLOW ME THE PRIVILEGE OF ESCORTING YOU TO THE MEAT DEPARTMENT?

I HAVE TO ADMIT, I'M GLAD I RAN INTO YOU, LANCE. I'VE HAD A LOVELY TIME.
IT'S BEEN MY MOST PLEASANT VISIT EVER TO THE GROCERY STORE.

OH YES I KEEP FORGETTING WE'RE IN A GROCERY STORE...
ORDINARILY, IT'S SUCH A DREARY PLACE.

CHARCOAL OLIVES
DOG FOOD SPAM
THAT'S HOW **I**'VE ALWAYS FELT...
REALLY? THAT'S INTRIGUING...

ROMANCE IS A FUNNY THING. I'M STILL GETTING USED TO THE IDEA OF YOU AND BETH AS A COUPLE...
YOU KNOW, THERE'S A CERTAIN ART TO IT. FOR EXAMPLE, I WON BETH OVER WITH MY SECOND GRADE MACARONI SCULPTURE

OH, YES. I REMEMBER. ONE SIMPLE, CHILDLIKE GIFT FROM YOU, AND OLD STUDMUFFINS WAS HISTORY.
YEP. POOR OLD ROD JUST DIDN'T HAVE THE KNACK FOR USING SYMBOLIC GESTURES.

MEANWHILE
I HOPE YOU WON'T THINK ME FORWARD, BUT I GOT A LITTLE SOMETHING FOR YOU.
...CHOCOLATE... ...HOW DID YOU **KNOW**?

SALLY, I HAVE A PROBLEM.
WHAT IS IT, BETH?
©88 Sam Hurt

I MET SOMEONE. SOMEONE VERY SPECIAL. I'M AFRAID RATLIFF AND I ARE THROUGH.
WOW. THIS IS SO SUDDEN! WHO'S THE GUY?
4-18

DO YOU REMEMBER AN OLD FRIEND OF ROD'S NAMED LANCE TROWSERS?
LET'S SEE... THAT NAME DOES SEEM TO RING A BELL...

SO. YOU'RE GETTING INVOLVED WITH LANCE TROUSERS NOW...
HE SORT OF SWEPT ME OFF MY FEET, SALLY.
©88 Sam Hurt

HAVE YOU BROKEN THE NEWS TO RATLIFF YET?
WELL, NO. YOU TWO HAVE ALWAYS BEEN SO CLOSE... I WAS THINKING MAYBE **YOU** COULD TELL HIM...

SOME THINGS YOU HAVE TO DO FOR YOURSELF, BETH.
YOU'RE RIGHT. THE PRICE OF FREEDOM IS THE RESPONSIBILITY TO DEAL WITH THE CONSEQUENCES OF THE CHOICES WE MAKE...
4-19

IT WON'T BE EASY, BUT YOU'LL BE GLAD YOU DID THE RIGHT THING.
AN ANONYMOUS LETTER MIGHT DO IT...

RATLIFF, OUR RELATIONSHIP HAS BEEN REALLY GOOD FOR ME.
OH, IT'S BEEN GOOD FOR ME, TOO, BETH.

I THINK YOU'RE ONE OF THE FINEST PEOPLE I'VE EVER MET.
WELL, YOU **KNOW** I FEEL THAT WAY ABOUT YOU...
©88 Sam Hurt

WE'VE SHARED A LARGE PART OF OUR LIVES, THAT WILL ALWAYS MEAN SOMETHING TO ME.
UH OH
4-20

...ALL OF WHICH MAKES WHAT I'M ABOUT TO SAY VERY DIFFICULT...
AIRRGH !!!!!
RIP

PLEASE TRY TO UNDERSTAND, RATLIFF- I FEEL REALLY BAD ABOUT THIS...
I'M TRYING I'M JUST A LITTLE SHAKEN RIGHT NOW...

YOU SEE, ROD WAS CHARMING AND WITTY. HE GAVE ME SOMETHING TO ADORE; TO CENTER MY LIFE AROUND...

...THEN YOU CAME ALONG. I EXPERIENCED RAW, ANIMAL PASSION FOR THE FIRST TIME. I LEARNED WHAT IT REALLY MEANS TO BE A WOMAN. BUT LANCE GIVES ME SOMETHING NEITHER OF YOU COULD OFFER...

...COORDINATING WARDROBES.
RATLIFF, WE LOOK GOOD TOGETHER.

SO BETH HAS A NEW BOYFRIEND? RATLIFF'S LOVE-LIFE IS ON A TRAIN BACK TO SIBERIA.
YEAH. HE'S -OH, **HI**!
LOOK, IT'S SALLY AND EYEBEAM...

SALLY, YOU REMEMBER LANCE, DON'T YOU?
YES. NICE TO SEE YOU AGAIN
AS BEFORE, DELIGHTED.

YOU WEAR YOUR HEART ON YOUR SLEEVE, DON'T YOU, SALLY?
LISTEN, THAT WOULD BE GREAT COMPARED TO **THIS**!
WHAT'S THE DEAL WITH HER HAIR?
SHHHHH... DON'T STARE.

WHAT'S THE MATTER, RATLIFF?
MY GIRLFRIEND. EVERYTHING WAS GOING SO WELL... THEN, **WHAM**! SHE MEETS ANOTHER GUY, AND IT'S ALL OVER...

THERE THERE. YOU POOR DEAR.
I'M GOING TO GO LIE DOWN AND MOPE FOR A FEW DAYS...
PAT PAT

IT'S AWFULLY TOUGH HAVING YOUR WHOLE SENSE OF WELL-BEING AT THE MERCY OF ANOTHER PERSON'S FICKLE HEART...

THAT'S WHY I WENT SOLID STATE...
DRINK TO ME ONLY WITH THINE INTEGRATED CIRCUITS...

HONEY, I'M HOME...

THE CASE THAT WOULDN'T DIE. AFTER ALL THESE YEARS, THE DARN AMBERCROMBIE FILE INVADES THE SANCTITY OF MY VERY HOME...
PLOP

HOMEWORK. WHAT A BLAST FROM THE PAST. WHAT'S NEXT, A POP QUIZ?
AHEM.

HELLO, EYEBEAM. REMEMBER ME?
HANK! I DIDN'T KNOW IF I'D EVER SEE YOU AGAIN. I DON'T THINK I EVEN HAVE YOUR CURRENT ADDRESS ANYMORE.

SORRY. YOU KNOW HOW IT IS. BUSY, BUSY, **BUSY**! BUT LUCKILY, I FOUND A CHANCE TO BREAK AWAY AND GET BACK TO TOWN JUST IN TIME.
JUST IN TIME FOR WHAT?

COME ON! IF I HADN'T SHOWN UP BY NOW, THIS WOULD BE YOUR FIRST BOOK WITHOUT ME IN IT.
UH, YEAH... RIGHT.
UH OH... THE GUY IS **SERIOUSLY** DISORIENTED ABOUT HIS SURROUNDINGS.

I'M ONLY GOING TO BE IN TOWN FOR A FEW DAYS, EYEBEAM. OK IF I STAY HERE AT YOUR PLACE?
THAT'S FINE. AS LONG AS YOU DON'T MIND THE COUCH...

THE COUCH? GREAT. I REALLY **APPRECIATE** IT. DON'T KNOCK YOURSELF OUT.
HEY, IT'S THE BEST I CAN DO, ALLRIGHT? WE DON'T HAVE AN EXTRA GUEST ROOM...

RIGHT. YOU ALREADY HAVE A GUEST UNDER EVERY BED IN THE HOUSE.
OH. WHAT WAS I THINKING?

THIS LOOKS LIKE A NICE SPOT...

OH, YES! I'LL SLEEP LIKE A KING DOWN HERE... I WONDER WHO'S BED I'M UNDER...

DO THE CHAIRS IN YOUR PARLOR SEEM EMPTY AND BARE? DO YOU GAZE AT YOUR DOORSTEP AND PICTURE ME THERE? IS YOUR HEART FILLED WITH PAIN? SHALL I COME BACK AGAIN? TELL ME DEAR, ARE YOU LONESOME TONIGHT?
?

I GUESS I'LL TRY ON THIS NEW NIGHTIE...

I'M NOT SURE MY HEART COULD TAKE IT. I BELIEVE I'LL SEEK ALTERNATIVE ACCOMMODATIONS...

SO!

I'M GOING TO TELL YOU **ONE** TIME. STAY OUT OF MY SWEETIE'S BOUDOIR!
LOOK, PAL- FOR YOUR INFORMATION...
HONEY, WHO ARE YOU TALKING TO?

I'M TALKING TO THIS MONSTROUS MENTAL MALADY HERE- THIS OVERGROWN NIGHTMARE- THIS...
I DON'T SEE ANYTHING...

OH. I GUESS YOU **CAN'T** SEE HIM. YOU'RE TOO WELL ADJUSTED, MY PET.
COME SIT DOWN, MY LITTLE MR. TRANSISTOR.

IF ANYONE EVER NEEDED A GLASS OF WARM MILK, IT'S YOU, CREAM PUFF.
"MR. TRANSISTOR"?
OH, SHUT UP. YOU'RE JUST JEALOUS 'CAUSE I GOT THE GIRL...

I REMEMBER THAT GUY. SAY, WHAT'S THE MATTER WITH HIM?
WELCOME TO "LIFESTYLES OF THE RECENTY DUMPED" HE'S BEEN STARING AT THAT WALL FOR DAYS...
SIGH..

AH. POOR, SUFFERING LAD. MY HEART FEELS FOR HIS. PERHAPS A CHANGE OF SCENE WOULD PEP HIM UP.
MIGHT BE JUST THE THING...

I LOVE MY WORK.
IT SHOWS, HANK. IT SHOWS.
GRMBLE... MUTTRR... WIMMIN!

CHOC 'N' FIBER
CALCIUM! -THE WAY NATURE INTENDED!
IF ONLY I COULD FIGURE THAT ONE OUT-THEN I MIGHT BE ABLE TO ASCERTAIN HOW TO WEAN THEM...

Ratliff's
Believe it or not
ON THE CONTINENT OF NORTH AMERICA, THERE ARE BUSINESS ESTABLISHMENTS THAT SERVE SUCH ITEMS AS COFFEE AND BRAN MUFFINS, BUT REFUSE TO PROVIDE A PUBLIC RESTROOM!
SORRY.
THIS IS A JOKE, RIGHT?
OUTRAGEOUS BUT TRUE!

WELL, EYEBEAM, I MUST BE OFF AGAIN. TALLY HO.
WHY DO YOU HAVE TO LEAVE, HANK?
©88 Sam Hurt

BUSINESS. THE FIRST INTERNATIONAL **POIBLE** CONFERENCE IS COMING UP IN JUNE.
"POIBLE"?
5-9

PROFESSIONAL ORGANIZATION OF IMAGINARY BEINGS LACKING EXISTENCE
HEY, I KNOW A CONVENTION CENTER THAT WOULD BE PERFECT.

THAT WAS A **GOLDEN OLDIE** FROM WAY BACK IN '83 - OR WAS IT **63**? ANYWAY, "LET'S GRUNT" BY FLORESCENT RALPH. ROCKIN OUT HERE ON K-99, YOUR FRENZIED FREQUENCY...

HEY-TONIGHT AND **EVERY** TUESDAY NIGHT AT SLUGS, IT'S "DUMP NIGHT" ALL YOU GUYS WHO'VE BEEN DITCHED COME LEAVE YOUR CARES BEHIND WITH 2 FOR 1 DRINK SPECIALS...
NOW, WHO WOULD GO TO A PLACE LIKE THAT?
©88 S. HURT

SLUGS
5-10

LANCE- THESE LAST FEW WEEKS HAVE BEEN SHEER BLISS...
I'VE HAD A DELIGHTFUL TIME, MYSELF, BETH.
©88 Sam Hurt

I JUST HOPE MY FORMER BEAU RATLIFF DOESN'T GET BITTER ABOUT THIS AND CAUSE AN UGLY SCENE.
DON'T WORRY BETH. THERE'S AN UNWRITTEN CODE OF GOOD SPORTSMANSHIP AMONG FELLOWS IN THESE SITUATIONS.
5-11

LEMMEE SEE..
"FOR A GOOD TIME, CALL ZELDA JONES- 663-2947."
HERE-TAKE A FEW MORE FOR YOUR FRIENDS.
WHERE DID YOU HAVE THESE DONE?
YEAH. NICE PRINT JOB..

EYEBEAM
RATLIFF - WHAT ARE YOU DOING?
MOPING, SALLY. I'VE BEEN DOING A LOT OF GOOD, HARD MOPING, AND I THINK I'VE ALMOST MOPED THROUGH THIS CRISIS.
OH. YOU MEAN LOSING BETH.
I NOW REALIZE THAT MY LIFE HAD MEANING **BEFORE** BETH, SO IT COULD THEORETICALLY HAVE AN INFINITESIMAL LITTLE CRUMB OF MEANING AGAIN SOMEDAY.
SAY, THAT MOPING HAS REALLY BROUGHT YOU A LONG WAY IN JUST TWO WEEKS!
IT'S BUILDING CHARACTER, TOO. I CAN TELL!

HEY, RATLIFF - I KNOW IT'S DIFFICULT, LOSING YOUR SWEETIE, BUT IT'S TIME TO SNAP OUT OF IT.
COME ON - JOIN THE LAND OF THE LIVING.
THAT'S EASY FOR YOU TO SAY. WHAT HAVE **YOU** EVER LOST?
LET'S SEE... HUSBANDS... CATS... THE STUDEBAKER...
NOT NECESSARILY THE SMARTEST QUESTION I EVER ASKED...

GRANDMA X- I'M SORRY I MADE YOU SO DOWN IN THE DUMPS. I WAS ONLY THINKING OF MY OWN PROBLEMS... COME ON- LET'S GO TO WORK!

I HAVE THE CAR ALL READY. WE CAN STILL MAKE IT IN TIME. YOU WERE EXACTLY RIGHT. AFTER A CERTAIN POINT, IT'S TIME TO GET ON WITH YOUR LIFE... C'MON... PLEASE?

...IT'S REALLY A PRETTY GOOD JOB-FREE COFFEE ALL DAY. HEY- YOU MADE ANOTHER LIGHT!
WORKS EVERY TIME...

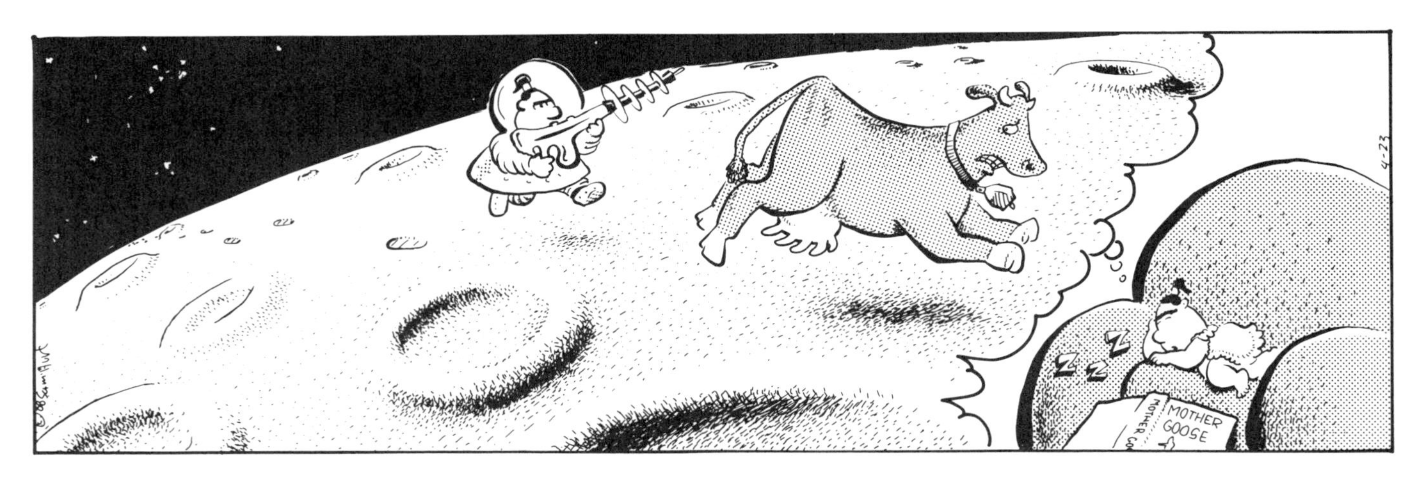
MOTHER GOOSE

BOOTH-FEST '88
CARICATURES $6
CRAFTS
DO-DADS

"THE KING"
GRANDMA MOSES
CUTE MUGS

"Couch Jockey"

LOOK, SALLY I HAD A CARICATURE DONE.
OH, THAT DOESN'T CAPTURE YOU AT **ALL**, RATLIFF!
"Couch Jockey"
©88 SAM HURT
COME INTO MY STUDIO. I'M GOING TO CAPTURE YOUR **TRUE** ESSENCE.
OK!
LATER
HOLD STILL.
IS IT ART YET?

MY ART IS VERY REWARDING, BUT IT DOESN'T PAY THE BILLS...
MY JOB PAYS THE BILLS, BUT IT DOESN'T LEAVE ME MUCH TIME FOR MY ART.
©88 Sam Hurt
BRAND X
ATTORN
THERE ARE OTHER JOBS I COULD GET THAT WOULD PAY BETTER, BUT THEY'D LEAVE **NO** TIME FOR ART.
I GUESS I NEED MORE CAREER ALTERNATIVES...
the PULSATING PETUNIA
CLASSY ADULT ENTERTAINMENT
HELP WANTED

NO!
I'M JUST THINKING THE IDEA OVER, RATLIFF...
SALLY, I'VE BEEN TO BACHELOR PARTIES AT THOSE PLACES. YOU WOULDN'T **LIKE** DANCING THERE.
I'M NOT THRILLED AT THE IDEA, BUT IT MIGHT BE THE ANSWER TO MY CASH FLOW WOES.
LOOK, IF THAT'S THE ONLY PROBLEM, PERHAPS I CAN-
OH, RATLIFF- THANKS, BUT I COULDN'T...
OH. I KEEP FORGETTING ABOUT THIS RECESSION THING...
A NOBLE GESTURE KNOWS NO ECONOMIC CLIMATE...

EYEBEAM, HOW CAN YOU JUST SIT CALMLY BY LIKE THIS?
WHAT DO YOU MEAN?

I MEAN, WITH YOUR GIRLFRIEND SALLY ABOUT TO BECOME A TOPLESS DANCER...

WELL, WHAT ARE YOU GOING TO DO?
I DON'T THINK THERE'S ANYTHING I **CAN** DO. I WOULDN'T BE HELPING THE SITUATION BY TELLING HER WHAT TO DO WITH HER OWN BODY...

WELL!...
...HE'LL NEVER SOLVE ANY OF LIFE'S PROBLEMS WITH **THAT** APPROACH...

WELL, HERE I AM. BACKSTAGE AT AN EROTIC DANCE CLUB. WHAT AM I **DOING** HERE? OH, YEAH. I NEED THE MONEY TO HELP WITH MY ART CAREER...
the Pulsating Petunia
• CLASSY • ADULT • ENTERTAINMENT •
C'MON, SALLY- YOU CAN DO IT. YOUR BODY IS A NATURAL, HEALTHY THING. ALL YOU HAVE TO DO IS WIGGLE IT AROUND FOR A BUNCH OF STRANGERS.
HERE GOES!
I GUESS THERE'S NOTHING I COULD SAY TO MAKE YOU CHANGE YOUR MIND...

SALLY, I STILL DON'T THINK THIS IS RIGHT FOR YOU.
I APPRECIATE YOUR CONCERN, RATLIFF, BUT I'VE MADE UP MY MIND...
YOUR **MIND**! THAT'S WHAT I'M CONCERNED ABOUT! YOU HAVE SUCH A GREAT **MIND** THAT THIS WOULD-
HERE GOES.
MY MIND, ON THE OTHER HAND, MIGHT BE READY FOR A 60,000 MILE CHECKUP...

AL**RIGHT**! SALLY, YOU'RE NOT A TOPLESS DANCER AFTER **ALL**!
I BEG YOUR PARDON.
WELL, I HAD THIS DREAM. YOU NEEDED THE MONEY, SO YOU GOT A JOB DANCING AT THE "PULSATING PETUNIA"
MMM... AND I TAKE IT YOU WERE THERE?
I **HAD** TO GO IN. I WAS TRYING TO TALK YOU OUT OF THE WHOLE THING...
AND HOW MANY OTHER DREAMS HAVE YOU HAD WHERE I ENDED UP UNDER-ATTIRED?
ABOUT FIFTY OR SIXTY, BUT IT WAS ALWAYS RELEVANT TO THE PLOT.
I OUGHT TO AT LEAST HAVE SCRIPT APPROVAL...
EYEBEAM

EYEBEAM
EYEBEAM, HAVE YOU HEARD OF THE CONCEPT CALLED "ANTHROPY"?
I DON'T THINK SO, RATLIFF...
IT'S THE IDEA THAT WITHOUT MAN HERE TO OBSERVE THEM, CERTAIN PHENOMENA OUT THERE IN THE UNIVERSE WOULDN'T EXIST...
I DON'T KNOW... SOUNDS A BIT **FAR-FETCHED** TO ME.
©87 Sam Hurt
WHAT DO **YOU** THINK, SALLY?
WHAT'S THAT? I'M SORRY... I WASN'T LISTENING.

EYEBEAM
TEETER
WHA?
TOTTER
©87 Sam Hurt
OOOH...
GAH-
WHUMP
THE CONTENENTAL SHELF MUST HAVE SHIFTED AGAIN...
SPLAH!

SALLY, COULD YOU WATCH PEACHES AND HER BROTHER, TYKIE FOR A WHILE?
WELL, I-
I DON'T **NEED** A BABYSITTER. I'M TOO **OLD**!
©88 Sam Hurt
SEE, I HAVE TO RENEW MY DRIVER'S LICENSE... PEACHES HAS HER TOY, G.I. JOSEPHINE.
ACTUALLY, I-
SOME TOY. SHE DOESN'T MOVE, TALK OR FOLD, AND HER HAND GRENADES ARE **FAKE**.
...AND HERE'S TYKIE'S STUFF...
I'M SORRY, RATLIFF, BUT-
IT'S A CRAZY THOUGHT, REALLY A BABYSITTER FOR THE QUEEN OF THE UNIVERSE.
LUVS
PAMPERS
3-28
WELL, I GUESS IT'S THE LEAST I CAN DO...
DOWN ON YOUR **KNEES**, PEASANT!
LUVS
PAMPERS

HELP CALL POLICE
HELP CALL POLICE
HELP CALL POL
HELP CALL POLICE
HELP CALL
©87 Sam Hurt

I'VE GOT TO FIND SOMEONE TO LOOK AFTER TYKIE FOR A WHILE...
©88 Sam Hurt

I CAN'T ASK SALLY. SHE HELPED ME OUT YESTERDAY... EYEBEAM'S AT WORK...
OH- IS THAT THE LITTLE BABY? I JUST LOVE LITTLE BABIES.

I LOVE THEIR LITTLE FACES! I LOVE THEIR TEENIE WEENIE LITTLE FEET! I LOVE THEIR ITTY-BITTY LITTLE HANDS...
3-29

I EVEN LOVE CHANGING THEIR LITTLE DIAPERS...
GRANDMA X, I AM ABOUT TO MAKE YOU A VERY HAPPY WOMAN...

WELL- IF IT ISN'T THE LITTLE SNAKE WHO STOLE MY GIRL!
OH, HI, ROD..., HAVE A SEAT...
©88 Sam Hurt

BUT SERIOUSLY- HOW ARE YOU AND THE LITTLE EX GETTING ALONG?
THEN, YOU HAVEN'T HEARD...
FRIENDLY SHOVE

UH-OH. SOUNDS LIKE YOU HAVE AN ANNOUNCEMENT. WELL, GET IT OVER WITH. I HAVE A STRONG EGO. I CAN TAKE IT.
SHE LEFT ME FOR YOUR OLD SCHOOL BUDDY, LANCE TROUSERS.
5-26

LANCE TROUSERS !?
YEAH. YOU REMEMBER HIM. DARK HAIR. GOOD DRESSER. ALWAYS THE SAME SIZE.

LANCE TROUSERS AND BETH. TOGETHER. SO IT FINALLY HAPPENED.
ROD, I'M SURPRISED THIS BOTHERS YOU SO MUCH. AFTER ALL, BETH LEFT YOU FOR ME A LONG TIME AGO.
5-30

WELL, THAT DIDN'T EXACTLY MAKE MY DAY... BUT, THIS- THIS IS LIKE THE FULFILLMENT OF SOME DARK PROPHECY FROM THE PAST...
IT IS?
©88 Sam Hurt

EVER SINCE I'VE KNOWN LANCE, I'VE BEEN LOOKING OVER MY SHOULDER. WHEN I SEIZE A NEW TROPHY ON THE PLAYING FIELD OF LOVE, I'M ALWAYS AFRAID HE'LL COME ALONG AND INTERCEPT HER. WELL, IT FINALLY HAPPENED!
OH. SO I WAS JUST RUNNING INTERFERENCE.

HEY, RATLIFF- COME BACK! I DIDN'T MEAN TO DISCOUNT THE EFFECT OF THIS WHOLE MESS ON YOUR EMOTIONS... HOW ARE YOU TAKING ALL THIS?

OH, I'M GETTING OVER IT. I GUESS MY SELF IMAGE NEVER ALLOWED ME TO BELIEVE BETH WAS EVER MINE IN THE FIRST PLACE.
I'VE WONDERED ABOUT THAT. WHAT IS YOUR SELF IMAGE, ANYWAY?
©88 Sam H.

I SEE MYSELF AS A GLOB OF MASHED POTATO ON THE LINOLEUM COUNTERTOP OF LIFE...

PALS ?
SURE.
CLINK
YOU KNOW, WHEN TWO GUYS HAVE BEEN DUMPED BY THE SAME GIRL, IT CREATES A CERTAIN BOND...
I GUESS WE NOW SHARE AN EXPERIENCE THAT'S UNIQUE TO US...
SLAP

THAT MAKES US BETTER BUDDIES THAN WE EVER WERE BEFORE.
YEAH!

OF COURSE, IF IN THE FUTURE WE WERE EVER TO COMPETE FOR THE SAME WOMAN, I'D **STILL** HAVE TO KILL YOU...
HEY, A BUDDY UNDERSTANDS THESE THINGS.

FINANCIAL
STOCKS
WORLD NEWS
LIFESTYLE

LOOK! HE'S DOING IT AGAIN!
COME SEE, RATLIFF. HE'S MAKING THIS PERFECT LITTLE ELVIS SMILE!
AGAIN? OH, GREAT!
PAMPERS
HUGGIES
LUVS

I THINK A TRIP TO THE BEACH WILL BE FUN...
YEAH, BUT I HOPE WE HAVE ENOUGH MONEY WHEN WE GET THERE.
6-2 ©88 Sam Hurt
OH? WHY ARE YOU WORRIED ABOUT THAT?

OUR GAS MILEAGE HASN'T BEEN TOO GREAT.

HEY, EYEBEAM- HAVE YOU EVER NOTICED HOW PATTERNS IN NATURE SEEM TO BE REFLECTED ON DRASTICALLY DIFFERENT SCALES?
YOU MEAN LIKE THE SPIRAL SHAPE OF OUR GALAXY AND THE WHIRLPOOL IN YOUR KITCHEN SINK?
©88 Sam Hurt

WOW... THAT'S A **GOOD** ONE...
6-3

AS QUEEN OF THE UNIVERSE, I LOVE VISITING THE EXOTIC OCEAN PLANET, MERA. I'VE ALREADY SPOTTED THREE MIGRATORY BOX-DWELLERS...
...THE RICH VARIETY OF LIFE HERE NEVER CEASES TO AMAZE ME. LOOK- THERE GOES A WHEEL-FOOTED TUNEHEAD. THEY USED TO BE HUNTED FOR SPORT...
6-4 ©88 Sam Hurt

AND OF COURSE YOU CAN SOMETIMES FIND MORE FAMILIAR LIFE FORMS...

SO...VACATIONING ON THE BEACH?
YES, O QUEEN.
DON'T MESS W
©88 Sam Hurt

THIS IS GREAT. THE TRIKE CLUB CAN RIDE AGAIN! WE'LL CONQUER THIS STRANGE LAND.
BUT WE DON'T HAVE OUR TRIKES WITH US, O QUEEN.

6-6

HEAR IT, MEN? -THAT RATTLING, SQEAKING SOUND? THE ENEMY SUB IS VERY CLOSE. I CAN FEEL IT OUT THERE. TWO DEGREES TO PORT.
YES, CAPTAIN.
Squeeee Screeee squeee

CAPTAIN- REQUEST PERMISSION TO USE SONAR TO LOCATE ENEMY SUB.
DENIED. WE DON'T WANT THEM TO HEAR **US.** 2° LEFT, NO ENGINE...
PSSST... YES, CAPTAIN...
©88 Sam Hurt

THAT'S RIGHT, BOYS. JUST LET HER DRIFT... I HEARD IT A MINUTE AGO. IT'S REAL CLOSE. MAINTAIN SILENCE... WE'LL JUST WAIT THEM OUT...

... SILENCE...
6-7

AIGH!
PSSST- CAPTAIN- I **HEARD** IT THAT TIME...
IF ONLY WE HADN'T BLOWN ALL OUR TORPEDOS ON THAT SCHOOL OF GROUPER!

I'M GLAD WE DID THIS. IT'S GREAT TO GET AWAY FROM IT ALL.
BEING NEAR THE WATER IS KINDA THERAPEUTIC. I THINK IT'S BEEN ESPECIALLY GOOD FOR RATLIFF.

YEAH - HE WAS PRETTY BLUE ABOUT LOSING BETH TO LANCE TROUSERS...
I SAW HIM JUST NOW. I THINK ALL THE SUN AND WATER IS BRIGHTENING HIS OUTLOOK.
©88 Sam Hurt
6-9

EYEBEAM
NICE TO BE WET.
YEAH... IT'S A SCARY KIND OF FUN.
©88 Sam Hurt
SCARY?
WELL, MY MIND ALWAYS PLAYS TRICKS ON ME. YOU KNOW- HUGE SEA- CREATURES IN THE WATER ALL AROUND ME...
OH, YES... THE MIND IS FUNNY THAT WAY...
AH-HA! SO I'M NOT THE ONLY ONE...
GREAT. NOW SHE'S GOT ME DOING IT...

EYEBEAM
HANK! I DIDN'T KNOW YOU TAGGED ALONG ON THIS TRIP...
USE YOUR HEAD, EYEBEAM. IF I'M A FIGMENT OF YOUR UNCONSCIOUS MIND, HOW FAR BEHIND COULD I BE?
BUT WHAT ABOUT ALL THOSE OUT-OF-TOWN TRIPS YOU TAKE?
RAMBLINGS OF YOUR IMAGINATION.
©88 Sam Hurt
SO, YOU HAVE NO EXISTENCE INDEPENDENT OF ME? WHEN I'M NOT THINKING OF YOU, YOU DON'T EXIST?
THAT'S RIGHT. 'SCUSE ME. I GOTTA GO.
GEE... POOR GUY...
EEK!

EYEBEAM
THUNK
CLICK
©88 Sam Hurt
6-10

I THINK I'VE BEEN GETTING SOME GOOD SHOTS WITH MY 'WATERPROOF CAMERA...
YEAH. CAMERAS ARE GREAT. YOU CAN CARRY AN IMAGE AROUND WITH YOU FOREVER...
©88 Sam H
OF COURSE, YOU CAN CARRY AN IMAGE AROUND WITH YOU **WITHOUT** A CAMERA, TOO.
ANYWAY, EVERYBODY'S UP AT THE CLUBHOUSE. C'MON!

BY THE WAY, WHY AREN'T YOU TURNING INTO A LOBSTER LIKE THE REST OF US? ...SUNBLOCK?
- RATLIFF?

EYEBEAM

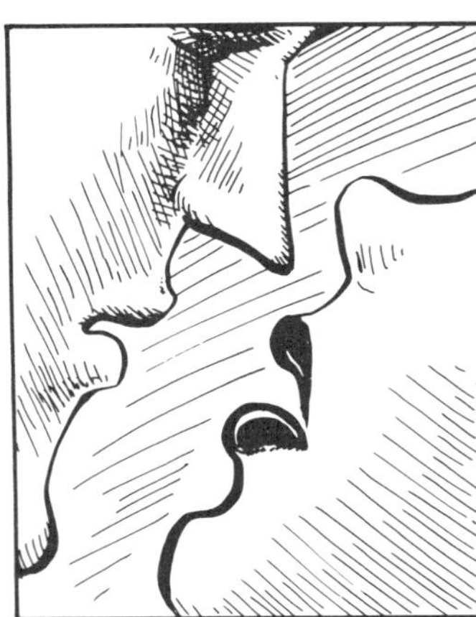

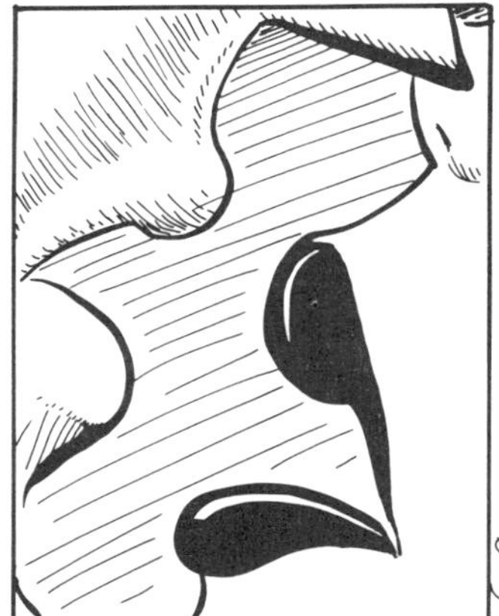

EYEBEAM

EYEBEAM

WELL, IT WAS A FUN TRIP, BUT NOW WE HAVE TO HEAD BACK HOME AGAIN...
6-17

KINDA QUIET BACK THERE.
I GUESS THEY'RE SAVORING THEIR MEMORIES OF THE TRIP...

HEY, BUDDY- COULD YOU SPARE $1:50 FOR A BOTTLE OF PERRIER ?
©88 Sam Hurt

THUDS
HAPPY HOUR
3PM – 2AM
THESE PLACES ARE A FASCINATING OPPORTUNITY TO OBSERVE THE AMERICAN PARTY ANIMAL IN HIS NATURAL HABITAT...
IT'S AN INTERESTING BREED, ALL RIGHT. THEY COME IN ALL SHAPES AND SIZES, BUT THERE'S A SUBTLE, INDEFINABLE QUALITY THAT'S ALWAYS THERE.
YOU MEAN THE INEXHAUSTIBLE, IRREPRESSIBLE, UNQUENCHABLE THIRST FOR EXCESS?
OH... MAYBE **THAT'S** IT...
DUDES !
6-20

RUN ALONG, GIRLS... **SHOOO** ! SIT DOWN, GENTLEMEN...
WE DIDN'T MEAN TO INTERRUPT ANYTHING, ROD...
NONSENSE. THIS IS LIKE FISHING... YOU HAVE TO THROW A FEW BACK IN ONCE IN A WHILE. FOR LUCK...
JUST AS LONG AS YOU DON'T CATCH OVER YOUR LIMIT...
WHO ARE YOU, THE **GAME WARDEN** ?
6-21

EYEBEAM
YOU KNOW, EYEBEAM, I'M AN IDEA MAN. AND IN TODAY'S MODERN JUNGLE, THAT'S A REAL SURVIVAL TRAIT...
AN IDEA MAN.
...TAKE POLITICS. TAKE THIS WHOLE ANTI-VICE CRAZE. IT'S REALLY GETTING OUT OF HAND. PEOPLE WON'T STOP PARTYING JUST BECAUSE SOME COMMERCIAL TELLS THEM TO...
IF I WERE FIRST LADY, I'D LIGHTEN UP MY APPROACH; GO FOR THE MODERATION ANGLE- URGE PEOPLE TO CUT DOWN SOME. I EVEN THOUGHT OF A GOOD SLOGAN:
"JUST SAY 'WHOA.'"
NEXT YOU'LL BE REPEALING THE LEASH LAW FOR PARTY ANIMALS...

SO YOU GUYS HAVE BEEN HANGING OUT HERE A LOT?
YEAH WE SHOOT POOL.. QUAFF A FEW...
SCOPE OUT THE BABES...
I GUESS THAT'S WHY PEOPLE COME HERE- TO LEAVE BEHIND THE CARES OF THE OUTSIDE WORLD...
RATLIFF..? ROD...? HELLO, OPERATOR- I'VE BEEN DISCONNECTED.

HEY, RATLIFF... HEY ROD... HOW MANY FINGERS AM I HOLDING UP? HEY, THEY'RE IN SOME KIND OF STUPOR!
BUT LET'S FACE IT, A STUPOR IS WHAT A LOT OF PEOPLE CAME HERE FOR... AND THESE GUYS ACQUIRED THEIRS QUICKLY AND WITHOUT GREAT EXPENSE...
©88 Sam Hurt
6-24
CAN I GET YOU ANYTHING HERE?
YES. I'LL HAVE WHAT THEY'RE HAVING.

©88 Sam Hurt
5-27

AND THERE YOU HAVE IT. WITH THE LATEST IN COMPUTER IMAGING TECHNOLOGY, WE ARE SEEING TYRANNOSAURUS REX MAKING A LIGHT SNACK OF WILLIAM F. BUCKLEY AND GEORGE WILL...
MUNCH MUNCH
JOIN US NEXT WEEK AS MORE FAMOUS JOURNALISTS ARE DEVOURED BY WELL-KNOWN PREHISTORIC CREATURES, ON "EAT THE..."
CLICK
YES, IT'S STILL TOO EARLY FOR A FIFTH NETWORK.
6-18

EYEBEAM
PERSIMMONS AND YOU
by Sam Hurt
New Stream Comics
HEY, EYEBEAM— SOMETHING HAPPENED TO MY BOOK ON PERSPECTIVE!
RELAX. I HAVE IT RIGHT HERE.

AFTER A LONG, HARD EON OF WISELY EXERCISING ABSOLUTE POWER, THE QUEEN OF THE UNIVERSE RELAXES ON HER THRONE.
SETTLING EVERY TURBULENCE IN AN ENTIRE GALAXY HAS BROUGHT ABOUT A DEVASTATING PEACE - A SILENCE OF AWESOME MAGNITUDE...
KINDA **QUIET** AROUND HERE TODAY...

THERE'S SOMETHING QUEER ABOUT THE STATUS-QUIRK AROUND HERE LATELY...
LIKE DINOSAURS AND ROBOTS HANGING OUT, EXCHANGING VIEWS...
OR LEARNING I AM GIFTED ON ACCORDION INNATELY.
USED JUNK
I'D **LIKE** TO SOLVE LIFE'S PUZZLES, BUT THERE'S TOO DAMN MANY CLUES...